Ashes Blown in the Wind

Ashes Blown in the Wind

Philip Antony

Ashes Blown in the Wind

Copyright © 2023 Philip Antony

All rights reserved

No part of this publication may be reproduced, stored in a retrieval system, or transmitted, in any form or by any means, electronic, mechanical, photocopying, recording or otherwise, without the express written permission of the author.

Acknowledgments

Perhaps one of the more challenging aspects of writing a book, apart from actually writing it, is the thankless task of editing. I was fortunate to have both a dear friend and the editor of this book: Moshe Banai, Ph.D. I would be remiss if I didn't recognise his invaluable suggestions to make this story a better read.

It is with enormous gratitude mixed with sadness that I acknowledge the invaluable contribution of Sara Jean who was my first and most critical editor; who helped me with the numerous re-writes; and who gave me the encouragement to continue to write not only this story, but many others. Sadly, she is no longer with me, and will be sadly missed as my best editor, best friend and life partner.

Contents

Chapter One

Paul Tressler could hardly contain himself. The flight was going to be delayed for two hours until 10:00 pm. In that interval, Tressler had two client calls and several FaceTime calls with the staff. Never mind that they had just put in twelve hours in the office. If Tressler was awake, everyone on the staff would be awake. The first-class lounge was buzzing with calls owing to the wait. He tempered his anxiety with three vodka martinis and an assortment of junk food. At 9:30 pm, the passengers were permitted to embark, with the flight attendants taking the brunt of passenger exasperation.

Within minutes of take-off from JFK in New York, the 747 behemoth leveled off, and the flight attendants in first class were quickly distributing champagne and apologies. Hopefully, this would assuage the passengers and help them forget the previous two hours in the departure lounge. Tressler waved off the champagne and ordered two vodka martinis.

After several rounds of hastily served drinks, the flight attendants proffered an elegant-sounding menu with a flourish befitting a *maitre d'hotel*. It offered "Poulet d'Orange Avec Pomme de Terre Gratinée" and "Fruits de Mer et Pomme Frittes." When the time for selection of one of these gastronomic-sounding delights came, the flight attendant asked perfunctorily, "Chicken or fish, sir?"

He had eaten, not so much from hunger, but rather because he had run out of things to amuse himself and to absorb his energy. He could only sit still long enough to speed-read two magazines, cover to cover, and watch a mind-numbing film on a screen only a little larger than a woman's compact mirror. His laptop batteries were long dead, denying him more time to play solitaire and chess with the computer. For the remainder of his journey to

Johannesburg, he found himself making repeated rounds of the jumbo jet until one of the passengers became annoyed at this man's frenetic pace around the plane. He tried unsuccessfully to lull himself into a demi-sleep state by drinking several more martinis, and staring out the window into infinity, alternately constructing images from cloud formations to imagining the people who lived out their lives on the green-brown patches several miles below.

Despite all the sophisticated infra-red landing detector technology, the jumbo settled with a jarring thump on the runway, and its engines roared angrily as the pilots reversed thrust to bring the plane to a crawl onto the taxiway at O.R. Tembo International. The pounding and the bone-rattling vibrations startled Paul Tressler awake from his self-induced comatose state, brought on by one too many vodka tonics, followed by too many minis of what was labeled 'Merlot.'

Paul Tressler was a self-made multi-millionaire at the age of 35, and by 40, he was the sole owner of a hedge fund with one hundred billion dollars of assets under management. He was also divorced, living in Soho – alone. He suffered from high blood pressure caused by either eating readymade meals or dining out – again, alone. His business, rather, his preoccupation with his business, precluded any friendships. The extent of his romantic life consisted of an occasional evening of frenetic sex. His staff described him as having "furious energy". His life was a series of daily façades, like kabuki masks fitted especially for Wall Street. He had compartmentalized his life, his feelings and emotions, and his relationships. To his therapist, he described his life as a series of highly organized but unconnected black boxes that gave Tressler the flexibility to adopt convenient personalities to promote himself or his business. Despite his quirky work habits, the late-night meetings, and a social life that was fueled with cocaine, and expensive wine, Tressler appeared to be reasonably fit and good-looking. He had a gregarious and charming demeanor that was practiced and rehearsed, but the underlying reality hid a complete lack of empathy for people.

Tressler's day began with a 7:00 am videoconference with his staff, and ended in the early morning hours that included dinner with clients followed by a nightcap – alone – at his favorite bar. His long-suffering staff endured the hellish hours and frenetic pace he kept only because he enslaved them as the best-paid financial serfs in the City, coupled with an iron-clad non-compete contract.

Today, however, was different. Tressler found himself on this night flight to visit a South African mining consortium with the sole goal of finalizing a deal worth at least $2 billion in the shortest time possible, and then returning to New York. He loathed traveling, especially outside the US, and had arguably an irrational fear of anything, including people, that he couldn't compartmentalize or reduce to something familiar and predictable or buy-off. At that moment, from the vantage of his window seat, Tressler tried to reduce South Africa and his impending visit to its lowest common denominator – a typical business deal with typically uninspiring, vapid executives in a typical glass enclosure hermetically sealed off from the real world. He concluded that, like his own country, South Africa was a nation with stunning beauty, social contradictions, unfinished structural development, and a complex historical racial divide that continued to persist just below the veneer of reconciliation.

As the plane came to a halt, the passengers jumped to their feet, eager to escape their sixteen-hour confinement. Tressler joined the beleaguered travelers to reclaim their baggage and submit to the indignity of border security on the other side of their journey. Although ludicrously expensive, the one advantage of flying in such an elegant style was that he wasn't subjected to the humiliation of gene-destroying x-ray searches or pat-downs by half-interested, underpaid border security agents at the departure area or the officious, sometimes hostile interrogation on arrival. The other perk of first-class travel was not having to queue in the taxi rank under the broiling summer sun of South Africa. Aggressive drivers haggled and jostled each other to attract exhausted economy-class passengers who wanted nothing more than to retreat to the relief of an overpriced but air-conditioned hotel room. First-class passengers, on the other hand, were provided an air-conditioned taxi, escaping the ubiquitous, black belching buses and cars that were held together more by prayer and curses than nuts and bolts.

☥

Chapter Two

Tressler's driver launched himself into the early morning traffic melee onto the Albertina Sisulu Freeway. Named after Albertina Sisulu, the 'Mother of the Nation,' the route to his hotel passed upscale neighborhoods, Edenvale and Modderfontein, with their fortified houses hidden behind high walls and iron gates topped with razor wire, complemented with shards of broken glass. It struck Tressler as bizarre that these homes were individualized 'green zones' in a social and economic conflict zone. They were supposed to convey the look and feel of a middle-class suburb, but instead, these fortifications spoke of an unbridgeable divide between the white elite and the grinding poverty and misery that was the reality just on the other side of those walls. These homes remained a stigma of South Africa's ugly past, and for many, its fictitious and failed efforts at reconciliation.

As the taxi driver swerved through the downtown traffic, Tressler began to feel that they were fleeing from someone or something rather than going to the hotel. As he slipped and slid from one side to the other in the back seat of the cab, he leaned forward to see the driver's license display as he went through every red light and stop sign. Alongside a photo of a smiling, bald-headed, and portly African, read "Zukile Kekana."

"Hey, Zukile, why the evasive driving tactics? Is someone chasing us?"

"Mnumzane, we stop, they attack us. If we lucky, they don't kill us."

"Who?"

"The gangs, mnumzane. Young guys – they have nothing, so nothing to lose. They steal anything and then sell it. Maybe, kill you too."

They arrived at the Hilton Sandton Hotel on Rivonia Road, much to Tressler's relief. He paid the driver 260 Rand, which included a tip that nearly doubled the basic fare. As a New Yorker, he knew that a good tip almost guaranteed the driver's availability for the next trip. As Tessler got out, Zukile looked back at his fare, "Mnumzane, this your first time here. Be careful. If you need taxi, sightseeing, massages, ladies, restaurants, Zukile knows Johannesburg good, and safe. You take my card."

"Okay, Zukile," taking the wrinkled and yellowed business card, "I'll keep that in mind."

A very thin young man wearing a faut-safari outfit that must have been worn by a previous doorman who was at least 100 pounds heavier stepped forward to open the door, "Welcome, sir, to the Hilton." Tressler ignored him.

Tessler entered the lobby. It could have been any lobby anywhere in the world. He could have covered the distance from the entrance to the check-in desk with his eyes closed. There were the same patronizing receptionists, the same bored porters and concierge. Even the guests resembled cutouts from central casting as they moved in slow motion to and from the ubiquitous lobby bar.

A porter swept up Tressler's bags and threw them on a cart without a word. He followed the man to the elevator, and when the doors closed, it seemed a signal for the porter to start his scripted elevator pitch delivered with a counterfeit smile accompanied by yellow-stained teeth.

"Mister, where you come from? American? How long you stay in Johannesburg? If you need anything, smoke, girls, fun stuff, you call Johnny? Okay?"

"Yeah, right; thanks, Johnny," but Tressler wanted only to get the business over with and get out of town. He handed the man a sizable tip that only confirmed to Johnny the Porter that there was a promising earning opportunity with this one.

Tressler thought about going down to the hotel bar, but then changed his mind. He remembered the many late-night trips that had ended disastrously. This one, too, would not come to a good end if he went down. He would probably wake up in the morning with a massive hangover next to a woman who looked breathtakingly beautiful in the bar, but would now appear haggard and worn. He took a long shower, trying to untie the knots in his muscles after his sixteen-hour confinement, and fell into bed. He had found the mini-bar and poured himself two large shots of cheap South African vodka that he used to wash down several sleeping pills. Despite the alcohol and drugs, however, sleep would not come. This was the beginning of his nightly confrontation with his demons. He fought off the faces that had both haunted him and denied him a brief respite.

Once again, in these terrifying dreams, he saw the nun to whom he introduced sex; she was crying and begging him to love her. He saw the smarmy executive who bribed him for inside information and who was then killed in a mob hit; and the countless lies and infidelities. There were the faces of all those defenseless and innocent victims that he had inveigled, cheated and used for his own selfish purposes. They believed in him, but after he sucked the life from their souls and their money, he tossed them aside like soiled toilet tissue.

He got out of bed and paced the room, hoping that his conscious mind could push those visions back into one of the many black boxes he kept hidden, but the faces lingered, refusing to accept his guilt as a token of contrition. After two more shots of vodka, the faces finally relented, and slowly disappeared.

He opened the curtains and stared into the darkness until the sky slowly turned from black to a dull grey, and then finally gave way to a pale orange – the sign that he had survived another sleepless night. He showered again and called for a pot of coffee. He was now ready for his day.

He found the wrinkled business card. "Hey, Zukile, are you up? I need a ride into town."

"Now, mnumzane? It's 6:00 o'clock in the morning."

"You want the business, or not?"

"Okay, mnumzane. I be right there."

Zukile hung up the phone, and cursed his good fortune. He had what was going to be a good paying fare, but had to leave the warm bed of his young wife.

"Where are you going at this hour?" his wife asked dreamily.

"To work, woman. It is no wonder that these abelungu die so young. These white people never sleep. Only work, work, work."

As he locked himself in his taxi, he peered into the early morning mist hanging over the street, shook his head and muttered again, "These abelungu, no wonder they die so young."

***

When Zukile pulled up, Tessler was already waiting for him. He jumped in and slumped into the back seat. Zukile could see from his rearview mirror that his passenger looked haggard. It was clear that he had not passed a good night, probably due to too much alcohol. He could not know that it was his client's fevered dreams that haunted him.

"Good morning, mnumzane. Where are we going?"

"Nedbank, Randfontein."

Despite several attempts Zukile made to break the morning gloom, Tessler replied only with grunts or the perfunctory "yes" or "no". Zukile had the radio on and was listening to a local DJ rambling on about South Africa's dismal performance in football that, in his opinion, was the reason for all that was wrong with the country, its leadership, and its role in world affairs.

"Do you mind, Zukile, turning that off?" It was not a request.

Fortunately, the morning traffic was headed in the opposite direction. Zukile was driving like an ambulance driver on his way to a hospital at breakneck speed, ignoring both traffic lights and the curses from other drivers as he weaved his way in and out of traffic.

They arrived at the bank with the screech of brakes nearly propelling Tressler into the back of the front seat. His briefcase hit the floor, spilling the contents. He didn't know whether Zukile was trying to make a point or he was just a maniac, but it didn't matter. He gathered up his things, stuffed them into the briefcase, and jumped out.

Tressler was hung over, sleep deprived, and hungry. This ride to Randfontein only made his dark mood worse. He regretted not passing this deal off to one of his analysts. *What was I thinking?* He asked himself. *This is a waste of my time. And, just because you wanted to see a gold mine? You're an idiot, Tressler.*

"Okay, Zukile, this won't take long. Wait for me."

Zukile didn't particularly like Tressler's style. There was no "please," no "thank you," but he knew that it was going to be a good day despite this distempered passenger – one customer and a very good fare.

"Okay, mnumzane, I'll be here."

Zukile found a place to park that was within sight of the office. It was going to be a beautiful day, one of those warm, dry days with a soft wind that blew off the Sahara. He turned on the radio to listen to the talking heads commenting on why the South African football team had such a dismal record. He muttered to himself, "South African government is like South African soccer – useless."

Tressler walked up to the entrance of the bank, and stopped. He took a deep breath. It was time to get ready for the meeting - to put his game face on – the charming but professional executive ready to do business. He squared his shoulders and opened the door to the offices of Springbok Mining and Exploration Ltd. They were waiting for him in a huddle in the executive conference room – the eight white members of the management team.

He chuckled to himself, "They're either afraid or need this scrum to make a decision."

It was clear to Tressler that this meeting had been stage-managed and scripted. Formal introductions were made, each accompanied by a proffered gold embossed business card. Tressler made a show of examining each card, but thinking to himself that the gold used in the cards would have been better spent on dividends. That will be the first change he would make after his investment. A team of white coats brought in carts overflowing with coffee, pastries, fruits and berries – enough food to feed a family of four for a week. Here was another change in the making: only store-bought cookies and coffee for future meetings. In between mouthfuls of malva cake, Tressler charmed his way around the room, after which pleasantries about the weather, children, and other banalities were exchanged. Then the squad of impeccably dressed dark-skinned servants, who had been standing at silent attention behind the tables, was summoned into cleanup service with an imperious wave of the chairman's hand.

Tressler listened patiently, feigning attention to the drone of monotone voices that accompanied the obligatory PowerPoint presentation, complete with a never-ending series of pie charts and graphs.

"We're in the Gauteng Provence of South Africa, Mr. Tressler, right in the middle of the world's largest deposit of gold. The Witwatersrand is a 56-kilometre-long north-facing scarp in the Gauteng Province. 'Gauteng' means gold, and approximately 50% of all the gold that was ever mined on earth has come from the Witwatersrand. Johannesburg sits on top of it. Our currency, the Rand, is named after Witwatersrand."

He felt himself being lulled into a stupor by the droning, monotone voice of the presenter; and mesmerized by the flashing slides. Together with the lingering effects of jet lag, too many vodkas, and terrifying dreams, he felt himself drifting off. He asked himself again what he was doing here. *Why am I putting myself through this? Why didn't I delegate this boondoggle to one of my staff?* They would have killed to make this trip; to get out of the office, and pretend to be important for a week. It was a few moments after the screen went dark that he heard someone, "Mr. Tressler. Mr. Tressler, are you okay?" Mercifully, the torture of the presentation was over.

"Uh, yes, sorry; just thinking about one of the slides," he lied. "That was a…very interesting. I'll need some time to digest this."

"We've arranged for you to tour our offices, and one of our mining sites just north of here. We think you'll get a better understanding of our business model."

Oh, no, he thought to himself, the obligatory site visit. He put on his best face, oozing charm, "That's very kind, gentlemen, but at this point, I think I need to spend some time with the documents." He lied again. "Let's fix something up after I digest this material."

He knew that there was no going for any site visit. He also knew from the research material provided by his staff that this company had the world's deepest hard rock gold mine at a depth of 12,800 feet underground. At such depths, the heat is unbearable for humans, and air conditioning is required for the safety of the workers. He had absolutely no intention of suffering through a day in the claustrophobic confines of a baking gold mine. "You're an idiot," he mumbled under his breath.

He excused himself and made a hasty retreat to his driver, who was now fast asleep in the back seat of the car.

"Hey, Zukile, wake up. Let's get out of here."

His driver startled awake, "Uh, okay, mnumzane. I'm ready."

Zukile told his passenger that the ride back to the hotel was going to take longer.

"Mnumzane, the R41, east to Sandton, is closed several miles ahead. Big detour. We need to take the long way on M77, through Soweto."

"Damn it, Zukile, I don't care if we have to go via Chicago; just get me the hell out of here! That's why I called you."

"All right, mnumzane. I'll do my best."

Zukile turned South onto Highway M77 without stopping for traffic signals for fear of the all-too-common traffic light attacks. No one else was stopping either. It was chaotic – horns blaring, drivers cursing, and screaming at each other at intersections. There were near misses and crashes; it reminded Tessler of the bumper cars at amusement parks.

As they drove deeper into the Soweto Township, the traffic began to slow and then went from a crawl to a standstill. The slow-moving cars were assailed by gangs of youths washing windows, then demanding payment; and women begging while two and three children clung to their skirts. Scores of residents came out in droves walking amidst the cars and hawking food, trinkets, and overpriced water bottles. Some cars eventually got overheated and were pushed off to the side. Those cars were beset by aggressive young men who swarmed over the vehicles offering the hapless drivers to fix, wash, push, or otherwise guard the stricken vehicle. It was pandemonium.

It was clear to Tressler that Zukile was no stranger to this melee. He waved, cursed, and screamed at a phalanx of window washers that descended on his taxi. "Don't you dare touch my car, you filthy scum! May UDeveli take your miserable souls to the nether world!

Tressler was surprised that this otherwise mild-mannered taxi driver could hurl such invectives. "Wow, Zukile, do you always get so pissed over someone touching your car?"

"Oh no, mnumzane, I know these boys; they are good boys. We do this ritual every day. It is a part of the drama of driving these streets, nothing more."

☥

Chapter Three

The route through Soweto was a road that led only to one destination: despair. The bumper-to-bumper crawl took him past the homes of the souls damned to the misery of poverty and hopelessness. In the glare of the sun, he could now see homes – if one could call them that – that were nothing more than wooden shacks with corrugated tin roofs to reflect the intense heat. However, the worst of it was the sickening smell of sewage running through open rivulets in the streets.

These ramshackle homes belied the pretense of reconciliation. It was instead the slow and insidious creation of an underclass of native South Africans. Here was the most virulent form of segregation: the parallel existence of separate races occupying the same space – each breathing the same air – but never touching. Beneath the veneer of reunion, there was a deep and impenetrable dark space between the white "Boers," and the black "Bantu" and "Coloured."

There was no way that Tressler could block out this scene that was a scar on the face of South Africa. He looked up to see Zukile looking at him in his rearview mirror. The driver's smirk told Tessler that he was getting a dose of the South African reality.

Zukile's South Africa was not just the much-vaunted glass towers and walled-off houses in Randfontein or Sandton. It was also Soweto, a part of Johannesburg – the known universe for many of South Africa's black population, including Zukile. Many were born here, lived here their entire lives, and, no doubt, would die here. This was his world. The only window to the world outside Soweto were the ubiquitous radios, a TV if one was really doing well, or the large screen TV in the local bar, or a computer in one of the libraries in Soweto. It was Zukile's world, but it was also a prison with well-defined boundaries. For others, it was like quicksand that would slowly but ineluctably suck one under. He told himself that one of these days, he would have his wife, Thabisa, teach him to use a computer. She was young – much younger than the middle-aged taxi driver. She was beautiful, bright, and had been educated at the Bhukulani Secondary School. For her part, her dream was to study to be a physician. Zukile was a lucky man, indeed.

Tressler endured the ordeal of the Soweto drive without a word. He nearly ran from the taxi to the front door of the hotel, where the same doorman dressed in the oversized safari jacket, complete with a pith helmet, held the door open. "Good afternoon, Sir. Welcome to the Hilton." He wondered how many times in a day that poor guy uttered those words, and only those words. And did anyone notice, or care? Tessler ignored him as he felt the blast of the cold air when he entered the lobby. He shivered momentarily from the cold tingling on his skin. He went directly to the bar, and ordered a large vodka tonic that was served up together with a bowl of bar chips that he would swear he saw last evening being pawed by a drunken guest in the lobby.

He found a quiet corner and began to go through the pile of documents he had received at the meeting. From a distance, he looked like a possessed concert pianist. His arms flailed as he tossed wads of paper in every direction discarding all but the financial statements. He was totally focused on the *pro formas*, oblivious to the waitress who came by several times to ask if he wanted another drink. He ran his fingers furiously up and down the columns. The conclusion came to him as if he had been struck by a bolt of lightning. He pounded his fists on the table. "What the hell were you thinking?" he said to no one in particular. "Deal? You call this a deal? You're a bunch of overpaid shitheads." He was shouting now. Heads turned, but he was oblivious. "This deal isn't worth shit!" How did he allow this to happen? Why was so much valuable time wasted on this deal? It was obviously going to fail. He could see it plain as day. Why didn't he challenge his analysts? He had seen some of the initial "teaser" documents, accompanied by a gold-plated key fob that was designed to resemble a gold ingot. Were they all blinded by a cheap bauble? Was he? Or, was it really something else: an unconscious desire to escape his empty life, to slow the blistering pace he kept with no goal in sight? Or, was it just simply to hide out for a while, to pretend that he was young again, and be free of the paternal mandate to succeed? He had no real desire to see a gold mine, or to associate with sycophantic executives looking to sell their business at the expense of the unsuspecting employees, or to sit through hours of rambling, testosterone-fueled negotiations. No, it's not going to happen; it was done. No further questions, meetings, or documents were necessary. It was time to get the hell out of this awful place and find somewhere more suited to his temperament. Perhaps, he would go to Monaco, where he could relate to the locals, where there was no racial divide or repression, or at least not an obvious visible divide. Everyone at the casino in Monaco was wealthy and oblivious to the travails of the world. This was his playground – where he was meant to be.

He gathered up the pile of papers and stuffed all of them in the bin at the end of the bar. He went straight to the concierge. "I would like to go to a restaurant, the best one in Johannesburg. What do you recommend?" The concierge's reply was immediate: a local place that served African food, good service, good wine list. "Make a reservation for me for 6:00 o'clock, and organize a driver," he commanded. He turned without so much as a "thank you," and left for his room. The concierge muttered under his breath, "Typical abelungu."

Chapter Four

He spent the next two hours on a conference call with his staff, voicing his disgust, complete with expletives, with the analysis of the gold mine play, together with what he perceived as a growing lack of energy and complacency.

"What the fuck are you all thinking? Any first-year MBA could have seen that this deal was just smoke and mirrors. Why am I paying each of you a shitload of money, not to mention your inflated bonuses – if this is what you consider your best level of expertise? I'll be back the day after tomorrow, and I want a deal review by each of you.

I'm not happy, people. I'm pissed off. I came all this way, and for what?"

He hung up, muttering that heads needed to roll. He poured himself a vodka from the mini bar, and took it with him into the shower. He spent a long time under the steaming hot water hoping that it would help to revive him after this useless meeting, and this equally useless trip. He decided that the staffer who recommended this business as a possible investment would be fired. "It was obvious on its face, you shithead," he said out loud. "How could you miss this?" It was going to be a long ride back to the US. A good dinner followed by an excellent bottle of wine would help to raise his sagging spirits.

His driver was waiting for him when he went to the door that was opened by the ever-present doorman whose greeting to departing guests was "Have a nice day." He could not comprehend how such a person could live such a banal and unfulfilling life as a doorman. Day in, day out — the same demeaning costume to evoke great white hunters, the same script, the same door. *I'd shoot myself,* he thought to himself. And yet, when he met the man's eyes, they showed no anger, sadness or apathy. Strange.

On the ride to the restaurant, it struck him that there weren't any people on the streets. There were streetlights and the evening was pleasant, but it was surprisingly quiet except for the sounds of the competing horns of drivers jockeying for position. The car came to a stop; the traffic was backed up. The driver looked in the rearview mirror and spoke to Tressler, "Sir, we are about a block away from the restaurant. It shouldn't be too much longer."

"That's all right. Just let me out here." Tressler hated sitting in traffic when he had nothing to do but watch a street roll by in slow motion, especially because of his earlier ride through Soweto.

"I don't think that's a good idea, sir. The streets are not safe, especially for a…" the driver hesitated, knowing that he had put his foot in it.

"You mean for a white person."

The driver stumbled over an embarrassed reply, "Well, sir, I'm sorry, sir, but it really…"

"Okay, okay. I get it." Tressler did not get it, or at least, not yet.

***

They reached the "Marble" restaurant at the end of the block on the corner of Keyes and Jellicoe avenues, but had to endure a queue of cars waiting to get directly in front of the restaurant. No one got out of a car or taxi until it was immediately in front of the restaurant, where the distance to the front door was not more than 20 feet. Again, there was the ever-present safari-clad doorman with a perfunctory greeting.

The restaurant was decorated in what was described in his hotel's glossy dining guide as a South African dining experience "in colonial Rhodesian style decor and service" – code for obsequious black waiters serving arrogant white diners. With a cleverly palmed $50 bill to the *maître'd*, he was shown to a dimly lit corner table. Although he had no particular reason for such paranoia, he always felt more comfortable with a clear sight line to the door, and of the other patrons. He was given a menu that was essentially a catalog of the animals that lived in Kruger National Park. A prospective diner was offered the opportunity to eat grilled chunks of virtually any animal that lived in that game reserve – from a crocodile and springbok to giraffe and zebra – all served on skewers. He elected a "sampler" of braised African game. He finished a bottle of red wine after drinking two vodka martinis, followed by a rather large snifter of South African brandy.

He paid his bill, handed out large amounts in tips, and walked out, or rather teetered out.

He stood under the cupola of the restaurant breathing in the cool night air that was mixed with the rancid smell of trash, sewers and grilled meat. It nearly turned his stomach as he stood waiting. He wrongly assumed that, like New York, there would be a taxi rank, or at least roaming taxis. After a long wait, he decided to walk, more to escape the overwhelming stench than out of lack of patience waiting. He had no idea where he was, where he was going, where his hotel was, or why he was walking, for that matter. He put one hand on the building wall to steady himself and then started walking, more like stumbling as the alcohol in his system took over his motor functions. The world in front of him was swaying back and forth.

Tressler hadn't walked more than 100 feet when there was no more building to hold to, and he fell sideways into the entrance of a narrow alley. His head hit the pavement, and for a few moments, he lost consciousness. When he awoke, he struggled to get up to all fours, but not before vomiting the contents of his stomach. His head was pounding; the world was spinning, and he felt a wet trickle on his cheek. He could taste the coppery blood and smell the vomit. He began to retch. He stayed in that position for several long minutes hoping that his head would clear.

♀

Chapter Five

Suddenly, he felt rough hands grab hold of him. Someone was pulling his hair and his collar, dragging him to his feet. Another pair of hands grabbed his arms. He was pushed against the alley wall and propped up by those hands. The one holding his collar produced a large blade, and pressed it against Tressler's throat.

"He stinks, baas."

A face appeared out of the darkness. It came so close to Tressler that he could smell the sweat and the foul acidity of his breath. It was a twisted face with a sneer that showed blackened teeth, and showered spit when he spoke. He eyed Tressler like a wild beast about to pounce on easy prey.

"Well, well, what do we have here? A rich abelungu? Are you a rich man? I think you are. You came from that devil pit where the rich Boers eat our animals, and are served by black slaves. Did you eat one of our gazelles, giraffe, rhino, eh, rich man? I think you need to pay more. Much more."

Tressler had never known real fear, the fear that comes from not knowing whether you will live or die in the next blink of an eye. Yes, he was afraid of losing a deal, terrified by the nuns in primary school, frightened at the thought of marriage, but this was different. This was primal fear. With the knife against his throat, and the dark menacing faces staring at him like hungry hyenas, Tressler began to understand mortal fear. Tressler's alcoholic stupor was now mixed with the sobering sense of his imminent death. These people didn't want money; they wanted revenge. He was going to be the token sacrificial lamb to right the wrongs of a whole sub-class who had been confined to a hell of poverty and exclusion. He could feel the warm urine dripping down his trousers.

"Ha, look baas, he pissed himself."

The dark, leering face looked down, and then looked into Tressler's eyes, and like any predator, he could smell the fear in his prey. "Cut him. I want to see him bleed, like our animals that he eats; just like our people are bleeding."

The man with the blade turned to face Tressler. He put one hand on Tressler's head, and the other blade pressed against his throat. The second man held Tressler's arms. Tressler's eyes were wide with terror; he was howling like a wounded dog. He tried to twist away from the knife but his head was pressed firmly against the wall, and strong arms held him fast. Tressler screamed as he felt the razor-sharp knife cut into his skin from one ear to the other.

"Slowly, slowly. I want him to bleed slowly. A quick death is an escape; he must suffer."

The knife-wielding man stepped back to assess his progress. The wound was not deep enough to sever the throat, or cut an artery, but blood began to pour from the cut.

Again, the dark man spoke. "Take everything from him. Leave him naked; take his underpants as well — nothing to protect his white arrogance. Then, kill him."

Tressler felt faint. He began blubbering and sniveling. "Please don't. I'll give you anything you want. I have lots of money, a car, anything, but please, don't kill me."

"You think this is about money, rich man? Yes, of course you do. All of you think that money is the balm to heal our wounds. No, I don't want your money. I want you to understand suffering, fear, and hopelessness — just like our people, just like the animals in the bush." They tore off all his clothes, emptied his pockets, and ripped the jewelry he was wearing. He fell to his knees, clutching his throat, hoping to hold back the blood flowing from his neck. They kicked and punched him without remorse, screaming, "Rich man dies, rich man dies!"

The dark man spoke, "Slice him. Slice him like they do with our animals. Then cut off his dick and stuff it in his mouth."

***

The last thing Tressler saw was the blade as it flashed in front of him. He knew he was going to die. He was too broken physically and emotionally to resist. He waited for the blade. But nothing happened. There was no final slash; the kicking had stopped. There was the sound of a scuffle, muffled grunts, and then silence. He was still alive, but afraid to open his eyes. When he did, he thought perhaps, he really was dead, and this was what his afterlife would be like for eternity. The three men who had accosted him were lying on the ground, very still. They lay in contorted shapes – like dolls discarded in the trash. Standing was another dark man who loomed above him like a black apparition. *I'm in hell,* he thought. *Is this what I have brought on to myself? Is this punishment for a wasted life?*

But this black phantom moved stealthily around the three men – like a lion examining its prey after a kill. Then, the wraith turned, and glided silently toward him. He slowly knelt down in front of Tressler. He brought his dark face within inches of his battered face. It bore thick scars and deep lines, more like a boxer after a brutal bout. His lips were full, but turned down. His eyes were deep, penetrating, and sad. Tressler raised his hands to protect himself when this black apparition reached down to lift him. He saw a pair of enormous hands that were gnarled, and were as large as his own head. Again, Tressler waited for the end – this time by an evil specter. And then, everything went black.

☥

Chapter Six

After a while, he heard a deep voice in his head. It sounded more like a slow beat on a timpani drum – a dirge for the dead. The terror returned; surely he was in hell. Tressler began to shake uncontrollably. He let out a cry of anguish. He was afraid to open his eyes. As he began to regain consciousness, to his surprise, the spectral voice was not menacing or angry. Strangely, it was soothing, almost soft. When he did, there was that face again, large, black, fierce, and yet…something was different. It wasn't the devil. It had to be an angel, but this angel wasn't the young, white guy with blond hair, and flowing white robes with wings that were the characters in story books, but rather a hulking, black man, bald, and dressed in black. A black angel?

"It's okay, it's okay. They won't hurt you anymore," came a raspy whisper. With that, the man gently raised him to a sitting position. He took out a ragged handkerchief and put it around Tressler's throat. "Here, hold this. The cut is not so deep; no arteries," came the dark-skinned angel's deep, hoarse voice. He gathered Tressler's clothes and gently put his trousers on him. Tressler was so undone that he could not move his arms and legs; they hung limply by his side. The black angel helped with the rest of his clothes. Although Tressler was dead weight, the big man effortlessly lifted him to his feet. It was only then that Tressler realized that this dark angel was no ordinary man. He had to be at least seven feet tall. Tressler was six feet, and found his head in the angel's armpit. But it was his size that made Tressler tremble and go weak at the knees. The man was built like a cartoon character of a giant come to life: his head, arms, hands and chest were enormous. He lifted Tressler with ease and began carrying him into the alley.

"What are you doing? Why?" Tressler passed out again before he heard the reply of this black angel.

He became aware that he was alive, or at least, he thought he was. He could hear a whirring sound, but nothing else. Although afraid of what he might see, he forced himself to open his eyes slowly. He found himself in a small room lit only by a bare light bulb in a lamp without a shade. Beyond the lamp, the room was dark; there were no windows. He was lying on a low cot with yellowed sheets. Alongside the cot was a fan that blew hot, fetid air in his face. He forced himself to turn his head and look around. Maybe, he wasn't dead after all.

Then he saw the dark angel sitting at the end of the cot, and for an instant, he remembered what had happened. He clutched his throat and found it bandaged with what felt like a plumber's tape. At least there wasn't any blood flowing from his neck, but the bed sheets were stained with large brownish stains of dried blood. The black angel looked at him, and Tressler began to shake in fear. "Please, don't hurt me. I can pay." Tressler's voice was hoarse, and he ached all over. He tried to move, but he could barely lift his arms.

The angel said nothing. He rose from his chair, and it looked to Tressler like a dark apparition was rising at the foot of the cot. Tressler put his hands up to ward off what he thought was going to be the killing blow, but then, he heard that same deep-throated voice he had heard in the alley: gentle, even comforting.

"I'm not going to hurt you. You were attacked in the alley. I happened to come along and stopped it." The black giant moved slowly, purposefully to Tressler's side.

"How long have I been here? Where am I?"

"Three days. You are in my home," was all the big man replied.

Slowly, Tressler's memory began to return. This was the man – the apparition - who stopped the attack, stopped three men from killing him. For a moment, he remembered the dark alley, the three men, and the knife at his throat. He then remembered three men lying very still, perhaps dead at this man's hand. He trembled as the memory of that evening began to surface.

"Who are you?"

The reply was throaty, almost hoarse, but soft. "My name is Bongani Okonjo."

"Bonga Okojo," Tressler stumbled. He found it hard to move his jaw. His lips were swollen from the beating and from thirst.

"No," Bongani Okonjo replied, "But you may call me Benjamin."

"Yes, Benjamin. You saved my life. How can I ever repay you?"

"You owe me nothing. You did not deserve to die. When you are well enough, you leave." Benjamin reached for a tin cup and offered it to Tressler. "Here. It is water; drink it." Benjamin held Tressler's head. His lips were parched and swollen from the beating. He could only manage a few sips before the water spilled from his mouth. "I will fetch some food for you."

Tressler's mind was in turmoil despite his beleaguered state. He was relieved and exhausted. For the first time since the "incident," he would call it, he felt hopeful. He fell into a deep sleep. When he awoke, he was startled to see his angel – Benjamin – sitting at the foot of the bed as before. He looked down to see that he had been bathed and, although naked, was lying between clean sheets. He remembered being covered in blood and his clothes that were soiled from the attack. At the foot of the bed were his clothes, cleaned and pressed.

"How long have I been asleep?"

"One day. I have brought some food for you."

With his enormous arms, Benjamin eased Tressler to a sitting position and proceeded to spoon-feed him. The smell of the stuff in the bowl nearly turned his stomach, but his hunger overcame any reservations about what he was eating.

"Thank you," was all Tressler could manage. It wasn't that he was not grateful, but rather, confused. Confused because he couldn't understand why this stranger had rescued him, and was now nursing him back to health. "Why, Benjamin, why are you doing this? I still don't understand. You risked your life for me. I'm a stranger to you. No one does that. You don't even know my name." Benjamin said nothing. He disappeared into the rear of the dimly lit room, and then returned with an ointment and proper bandages that he gently placed around Tressler's neck. It amazed him that the big man, whose hands were the size of a baseball glove, could be so gentle.

For the first time since he had been in the room, he looked around. There were no windows, just the naked yellow bulb in the lamp. Beyond the light, there was darkness. There was a chair at the end of the bed, and he could see what looked like a table in the shadows, but beyond that there was nothing. The air was thick and smelled like the inside of the local garage where he would have had his car serviced. The floor around his bed was tile that appeared to be stained from what appeared to be axle grease or engine oil. Definitely a garage once upon a time. Benjamin saw him looking around. "It serves my needs."

"Benjamin, I know your name, but you don't know mine."

"I know your name, Mr. Tressler. Your driver's license was among the things that were strewn on the ground in the alley. But your name is not important. Saving your life is more important."

"My name is Paul Tressler." He had to say his name; he needed to hear it out loud, re-establish his identity in this chaos. Benjamin said nothing. It would be another three days before Tressler was able to stand up without assistance. Benjamin had helped him with his first few steps. His ribs were still bruised, maybe broken. Breathing was difficult, and walking was painful. He managed to take several tentative steps with the aid of Benjamin, who wrapped his enormous arm around him and held him up like he was suspended from a cable. Several times, Tressler felt his feet leave the floor as the big man saved him from his faulty legs.

It was late in the afternoon. Tressler was seated at the table alone. Benjamin had gone to "fetch some food," as he called it. It was always the same: a stew with bits of mysterious purple-colored meat, slimy green vegetables and potatoes swimming in a watery broth. It suddenly struck the man that he had been in this "home" for the greater part of ten days with a giant of a man who had saved his life, nursed his wounds, bathed and washed him, and fed him. He had asked nothing in return, and his laconic style meant that other than his name, he knew nothing about the gentle, generous giant.

♀

Chapter Seven

It occurred to Tressler that he had not been in touch with his office, or with the South African mining company since the "incident". For all intents and purposes, he had disappeared. He felt a wrenching twist in his stomach. They must be in a panic. I've got to get in contact with them. He searched the large room for his cell phone. He found it where he had left it: in the left pocket of his torn sport jacket. He switched it on to find that there was still a charge. He dialed his office. On the second ring, someone answered.

"Tressler Investments, how may we help you?"

"This is Tressler."

"Oh, hello, boss. How is the trip going?" one of his analysts said cheerily.

It stunned him. He had been gone for almost two weeks, and instead of the concern, even panic, he thought most certainly would have greeted him, there were no expressions of concern about his being out of touch for so long. There were no calls from the mining company either. *If they were that keen, shouldn't they would be calling every day? No one really cared, did they? All they really want is my money. Did they dislike me that much? Yeah, I'm tough and demanding, but do I deserve this?* He felt a twinge of anger. *Damn it, they should all be grateful. I've provided them with a living, a good living come to that. And this is what I get in return – a cheery "hello"?* He caught himself. *Self-pity doesn't become you,* Tressler thought to himself. *Just be angry. There'll be a reckoning when I get back.*

"Tell me what's been going on," he nearly shouted into the phone.

"Nothing, boss. Same old, same old."

Tressler was about to explode in the phone when the door opened, and Benjamin walked in carrying food.

Strangely, Tressler's anger quelled at the sight of the big man. "Okay, speak soon," and he hung up. "Hello, Benjamin," he said as he turned to see Benjamin putting the bowl of broth with floating mysterious chunks of purple meat on the side table.

"Thank you."

Benjamin said nothing as he shuffled to assume his post at the foot of the bed. He looked tired and drawn. His shoulders were hunched, and his chin was almost touching his chest.

"What's wrong, Benjamin? Are you ill?"

Benjamin seemed lost in his thoughts, or was just ignoring Tressler. He took in a deep breath, held it, and slowly let it out as he turned to look at his guest. It seemed to Tressler that he was about to say something, and then after several long minutes, said, "It is nothing. You should return to your hotel in the morning."

Tressler woke up early. He found that Benjamin was already dressed, sitting in his usual place. The big man was slumped over in the chair, staring into space, lost in thought. "I have arranged for a taxi to take you back to your hotel," Benjamin said without picking his head up.

"Benjamin, I don't know how to say to thank you. You saved my life. At least, let me give you something to show my gratitude."

Benjamin turned to Tressler. His face was furrowed with deep dark lines, not from an injury, but it seemed to Tressler that those lines were from a deep sadness beyond his comprehension or experience. It was a sadness that seemed to have twisted itself around Benjamin's soul like a creeping vine. The big man walked slowly, almost painfully, to Tressler. The giant placed his glove-like hand on Tressler's shoulder and looked at him with eyes that seemed to bore into his soul. The voice was low and mournful, but always gentle.

"Goodbye, Paul Tressler."

♀

Chapter Eight

Several hours later, Tressler was deposited in front of his hotel. He retrieved his room key from the front desk. He found once again that there were no messages waiting for him, and there were no messages on his room phone either. Despite his complete lack of empathy, he still felt wounded by the lack of any contact from his office. He looked in the mirror and asked his image, "If you really don't care for them beyond being highly paid worker bees, and they know that, why would they call you? Why are you hurt?" He wandered around the room. It had the sterile and impersonal feel of a hospital operating room. This room was palatial compared to the ten days he had just spent in a hovel somewhere, but for some reason, Tressler found some comfort in that dark space. Or was it really the black angel, Benjamin, who transformed a squalid room into a home? It was this complete stranger who rescued him from certain death, tended his wounds, and then cared for him continuously without ever asking for anything in return. Who does that? Why?

Tressler was now alone. Before stepping into the shower, he looked at himself in the mirror. It seemed as if he had grown old in a matter of days. His cheeks were sallow; his lips were still swollen, and his left eye black and blue. He had lost weight and walked slowly and with a slight limp. Some of his teeth were still loose, and it hurt like hell to take a deep breath. The knife wound on this throat would leave a permanent scar. "At least you're alive," he said to his mirror image.

But, more than his wounds, he could not get the image of the black angel, Benjamin, out of his mind. Again, he spoke to the haggard reflection in the mirror, "Why, why would he do that?" That thought would not leave him. Selflessness was not in Tressler's lexicon. No one takes a risk anymore, not in this day, and certainly not risking your life for another. Trust, love, generosity and compassion were for Christmas cards and funeral eulogies. But the black angel had done just that – risked his own life – and wanted nothing in return. He had to know why. He had to get Benjamin to accept some token of his gratitude for his selfless act.

He thought long and hard. This really isn't about my gratitude, is it? "That's not it, is it Tress? You owe this guy, and you don't like being in his debt," he muttered. That's the heart of it. It was the man's refusal to accept a reward, and relieve him of any nagging feeling that he was beholden to somebody. Otherwise, it would put him in an inferior bargaining position – something that he never allowed both in his personal life and in business. That would be a millstone around his neck. "I always pay my debts."

But he couldn't put the thoughts to rest. Why? Who is this guy? He's not some religious, new-age nut. A Buddhist, perhaps? He's dirt poor, lives in a reclaimed mechanic's garage and yet, he fed me, cleaned my clothes, and nursed me. Why again? Over and over. The thoughts were like a stain on his shirt that wouldn't wash away. The more he thought about it, the more agitated he became.

He rummaged through the papers on his desk, and found the number for his taxi driver. After several rings, "This is Zukile."

"Zukile, this is Paul Tressler. I need you here now. I'll double the fare."

"OK, sure, mnumzane. I'm on the way. Where do you want to go?"

"I don't know."

"Mnumzane, you ok?"

"Damn it, Zukile, just get here. Get here…now." Tressler slammed the phone down in its cradle. He had to find Benjamin, his black angel. It was now an obsession. He would not rest until he had paid his debt to the big man. The thought haunted him.

Tressler rushed out to meet Zukile's taxi, and started talking even before the door closed. He related the events of the past ten days, especially the part about the restaurant, the assault and being rescued by Benjamin. Zukile listened, "Why do you want to go back, mnumzane.

You're safe in your hotel. Go back to America. Forget this place."

"No, Zukile, you don't understand. I need to find that man before I leave, and you have to help me."

Tressler retraced his steps back to the restaurant and the alley, but beyond that, he had no idea where he had spent the previous ten days. "Zukile, he lived in one room; it was a dump; the floor smelled of grease; there were no windows – just a bed and a lamp.

"Shanty Town," was all the Zukile said.

Zukile drove like a man possessed. He nearly missed the junction for Chris Hani Road, but jammed on the brakes, and turned hard into the junction. Tressler was thrown against the opposite door, and then back again to the other side when Zukile turned onto Nicholas Street. He came to a screeching stop in front of what some consider a carbuncle – a testament to decay and neglect, but to others, it was the heart and soul of Soweto – the Cooling Towers of the Orlando Power Station.

"Here, mnumzane, is the heart of Soweto. You must start your search here."

Once, the principal source of power for Johannesburg until 1998, the towers had been derelict and neglected for nearly a decade. Although, they no longer served their original purpose, the towers were now used for bungee jumping. They were painted in garish colors. One tower served as an advertising billboard, and the other contained the largest mural painting in South Africa. Tressler's mouth was agape as he looked up to see people jumping from a platform between the two towers. "That's nothing, mnumzane. They also jump into the towers. They crazy people." Zukile shook his head.

"Okay, Zukile, what now?"

"Now, you go into the streets and ask people."

♀

Chapter Nine

When Tressler looked across the street, he saw the maze of shacks with corrugated roofing, unpaved streets littered with trash, laundry hanging from windows and the random detritus from people who were too poor to care about beautification and less about sanitation, but who rather saw life as a daily existential struggle.

"No, Zukile, I'm not going in there alone, not after what happened to me last week. You're coming with me. I'll pay you 100 US dollars per day."

Zukile didn't hesitate. It was more money than he would see in a month, and then only when the tourists were in town. "Ok, mnumzane, for 100 US dollars every day, I come wit' you."

The unlikely duo spent the day wandering through the alleys and streets of Soweto. They negotiated the rivulets of dirty water running alongside the buildings, and the stench as they knocked on doors, or stopped a person to enquire about the big man. The description was always the same: a giant of a man, maybe seven feet, bald, big hands, soft-spoken whose name sounded like "Bonga Okojo," but called himself Benjamin. Most responded politely that they did not know such a person, and that Soweto was a big place with thousands of people. Others were not so courteous. The people of Soweto had long memories. It was not so long ago that they suffered through the brutality of apartheid. And for many, the scars were still very much in evidence. Although Zukile did the talking, the presence of a white interloper asking questions about one of their own was met with suspicion and hostility.

They continued for the remainder of the day despite the sweltering heat and the dust without an encouraging word. No one knew a "Bonga Okojo," or a Benjamin. Tressler had the nagging suspicion that people did know this man. Here was a seven-foot giant with a gentle and taciturn manner. How could they not know? Discouraged but determined, Tressler slumped into the taxi. "Zukile, take me back to the hotel." Neither Zukile nor Tressler said a word on the trip back to the hotel. "Here's your $100. Pick me up tomorrow at 10:00."

The second day was equally fruitless. They wandered through the northern portion of Soweto Township, from the dilapidated tin shacks to the more commodious cinder block homes, churches, a library, open-air fruit and vegetable stalls, and a variety of makeshift enterprises. Tressler could not help but sense that despite the evidence of generations of poverty, there was resilience here; life was teeming just under the surface. There was a hum in the air. He found it strange, almost uncomfortable. Notwithstanding years of repression and the continuing undercurrent of hostility, these people walked with dignity, their heads held high.

It was a long night for Tressler. After getting to his room, he sat on his bed, and nursed several vodkas before falling asleep well into the early morning hours. If it were not for the morning maid service, Tressler would have slept through his appointment with his driver.

He jumped out of bed, rushed through the lobby, and found Zukile waiting for him. Zukile quickly concluded that his $100 fare had not changed his clothes from the prior day. Tressler was unshaven and disheveled; he looked drawn, and his breath stank from too many vodkas.

Beyond his command, "Let's go," Tressler said nothing. Zukile thought to himself that it was going to be a long day. They drove further along Chris Hani Road, and turned south to Pimville Square, which served as the starting point for today's search. He stopped by the proprietor of the "Shoe Doctor," but had no joy. No one knew a man fitting Tressler's description with the name, Bonga Okojo, or Benjamin. As the day wore on, it became more evident to Tressler, and perhaps secretly to Zukile, that these people knew the identity of the man but would not disclose it to a stranger, an abelungu.

They walked along Modjaji Street and turned into unnamed side streets – more alleys than streets – knocking on doors and asking the same questions to passers-by – all with the same result as yesterday. Several times, Tressler fell faint as the effect of a hangover, lack of food and water, and the relentless sun that buckled his knees, forcing him to sit on a handy overturned bucket or on the ground.

"Mnumzane, you cannot go on like this. You will die," Zukile said. He put an arm around Tressler's waist as he faltered once again. He helped Tressler to sit on a bench in front of a tin shack. Five little boys laughed and shoved one another, playing football in front of him, oblivious to his plight. The sounds of other people, loud music, and the grinding, harsh noise of the township were overpowering.

"I'm all right. I just need a few minutes."

Suddenly, a large woman emerged from the house across the dirt alley with a cup of water in her hand. She had seen Zukile holding Tressler, who was stumbling. The woman wore a simple, pale yellow housedress and sandals. Her head was covered with a *doek,* a white scarf that signified that she was married. She walked with elegance and grace - and authority. When Zukile saw her approaching, he stepped back, and seemed deferential in his manner. She walked over to Tressler, bent down, and handed him the cup. "Drink this, young man. You have been in the sun too long; it is the ukuguliswa yilanga.

(sunstroke)" Tressler drank most of the water, and then dumped the rest on his head. He was about to thank the woman when his head started to spin, his eyes rolled, and he slumped backward.

☥

Chapter Ten

He awoke with a start to find the woman standing tall over him. She gently removed the towels from the back of his neck and his chest, and replaced them with cooler ones. He rose to his elbows, frightened by his surroundings, reminiscent of his earlier stay with Benjamin.

"It's all right, young man. You're safe. You need to rest for a few moments. The sun brings the ukuguliswa yilanga; it can kill a man, especially one with light skin." The only light in the room came from the front door. He could see three little children in the shadows staring at him. The smallest of them, a little girl with wide eyes and skin as smooth as brown velvet, approached him timidly, cautiously. She stood several feet from his bedside for several moments, then moved to her grandmother, and whispered something in her ear. Her grandmother smiled, and looked at Tressler.

"My granddaughter, Dumisani, is fascinated by your pale skin. She would like to touch you. Is that all right?"

Tressler was confused by such a strange request, but was too weak to resist. Truth be told, he was also intimidated by the woman's authoritative presence. He obliged. "Okay."

Her grandmother nodded, and the little girl approached him. Tressler amazed himself by reaching out to the child. He took her hand. Her eyes widened like little saucers as she stared at her dark hand in his white hand. After several long moments, she closed the distance to his bed, and climbed up. She put her arms around his neck and laid her head on his chest. Within a few moments, she was peacefully asleep.

Tressler could feel the child's rhythmic breathing. He didn't dare move. No one spoke. The other two children were now emboldened, and quickly moved to Tressler's bedside. They climbed on the bed, giggling as they ran their fingers through his blond hair. Zukile stood in the shadows, smirking. The woman looked at the hapless man who seemed overwhelmed. She smiled softly as she reached for the girls. "Okay, lokho kwanele (that's enough), you must let our guest get up."

"I am sorry, mister, but it is not often that children here see white people."

Again, Tressler found himself saying, "That's okay." *Maybe, it's the sunstroke, the "yilanga" thing,* he thought. Again, he surprised himself. "That's okay," he repeated. He swung his legs over the side of the bed. Although he still had a headache from the sunstroke, he knew he had to keep going. "Ma'am, I thank you, but I have to go. I have to keep looking for a man." Before he could finish his thought, the woman said, "Yes, your friend here, Zukile, told me. I believe his name is pronounced Bongani Okonjo. He is also known as Benjamin. Yes, I know him."

Tressler bolted upright and nearly fell over from jumping up, "You do? You know him, truly?"

"Yes, we all know him. In Soweto, we call him the Sangoma."

Tressler's heart was racing. "Where can I find him? He saved my life, and I need to thank him."

The woman scowled, "Young man, I can tell you, he does not want or need your thanks. He knows you are grateful. Benjamin is a very special person in South Africa. He possesses both gifts of a Sangoma and inyanga. As a Sangoma, he can read the signs and the omens; he can contact the spirits of our ancestors. He sees things in the sky and in the water that are beyond us. As umelaphi (healer), he can mix herbs that will cure the disease of both the body and the troubled spirit. He is a shaman."

"Please, ma'am, I must find him," Tressler pleaded.

"No one approaches the Sangoma, young man, without his invitation. I am sorry, but I cannot lead you to him. However, I will see that word reaches him that you wish to see him. He will decide whether he wishes to see you. That is all I can do for you."

Tressler realized that it was useless to argue his case any further with this woman. "Okay, will you let him know that I would like to see him, to thank him for all that he did for me?"

She nodded. "Wait here. I will be back in a few minutes." The three children dutifully followed their grandmother, leaving Tressler and Zukile in the dimly lit shack. For several long moments, neither man said a word. Tressler could no longer contain himself. He looked impatiently at Zukile, raising his arms, "What's this all about? I don't understand. All I want to do is say 'thank you' to Benjamin. What's all this mumbo-jumbo and mystery?"

Zukile walked over to Tressler, and put his face close to his. He had had enough of Tressler's petulance and arrogance. His eyes were bulging with anger; his neck muscles were straining, and his fists were balled up by his side. "Enough! How dare you! You call this 'mumbo-jumbo and mystery.' He saved your life. Isn't that enough for you? Why are you doing this?" Tressler's eyes gave him away. Zukile didn't wait for Tressler to respond, "This is really about you, isn't it? It is a feeble attempt to feed your petty vanity. This is not about your gratitude, is it? Once again, this is the white man, an abelungu, trying to use the black African to satisfy your pitiful needs, and fill the hole in your wretched life. You're pathetic, Tressler. I want no part of this deception." Zukile turned and walked out, leaving Tressler alone in the gloom.

Tressler was stunned. He suddenly felt very lonely; no, not just lonely but desolate. Every day, he was surrounded by clients expecting a return on their investments, fawning staff, or just strangers trying to ingratiate themselves into the pockets of a rich man. But, when he looked in the mirror in the morning, he was the only one there. No one really cared, did they? They're leeches trying to suck the life out of me. And then, he heard a voice, maybe inside him, maybe from the shadows, but it struck him like a thunderclap. "Aren't you just the same, doing the same thing, Tressler?" he said aloud. Before he was able to answer the question, the woman had returned, and was standing large in the door. Her expression told Tressler that she knew there was something unspoken hanging in the air.

"Benjamin will see you. I will take you to him." She looked around. "Where is your friend?"

"Gone," was all Tressler said, but by the look on her face, she sensed the turmoil.

"Come, young man, walk with me."

They walked for some way in silence. Tressler was angry, confused and just lost. *Why did Zukile speak to me that way? What did I do that was so bad? Okay, so I said, 'mumbo jumbo.' Where the hell does he get off judging me? Yeah, I'm white — petty, vain, and all that other bullshit. And he's black — downtrodden African, used and abused. What am I missing here? I don't understand. Am I supposed to feel guilty?* The questions kept coming, and the feelings made the questions more complicated. The woman interrupted his thoughts.

"Parsnips and eggplant."

"What?"

"Parsnips and eggplant. You are a parsnip; I am an eggplant. A parsnip is white; the skin of an eggplant is dark. Each of us starts as a seed that is nourished with love. You are the white fruit; and I am the dark fruit."

"I don't understand."

"You will, young man, soon you will."

☥

Chapter Eleven

It was getting late in the afternoon when they approached what seemed like a small park with a lone bench in one corner. Unlike his previous surroundings, this postage stamp spot had two large potted trees, green grass and a small plot of beautiful flowers. The woman gestured toward the bench. They sat next to one another in silence for a few moments.

"My name is Osumare Mashaba."

"Tressler, Paul Tressler."

"Tell me, Mr. Tressler, why do you really wish to see Benjamin? What is your real purpose, and why is it so urgent?"

"He saved my life, Mrs. Mashaba, and I just want to thank him. That's all. Zukile made it sound like this was more about white - black servitude and repression. What's wrong with saying, 'thank you?'"

For long minutes, the woman looked hard at him, her body rocking slowly like a judge deliberating before sentencing. She said nothing. Tressler felt her eyes boring into him. He knew, rather felt, that she could see through the thin veneer to the truth. "Okay, so it's not about gratitude. He made me feel inferior."

"Zukile *made* you feel inferior, Mr. Tressler?" She emphasized, "made." "A black man, a humble taxi driver, in South Africa *made* you feel inferior? Really?" Tressler saw a flash of disdain in her eyes. Before he could even frame a limp reply, she said, "No, Mr. Tressler, Zukile did not make you do or feel anything. It is your fear."

Tressler cut her short, "I'm not afraid of Zukile or Benjamin."

Mrs. Mashaba met Tressler's vain attempt at bravado. "No, Mr. Tressler, not fear of them. Benjamin makes you feel the fear of facing yourself. His eyes are mirrors. When you looked into his eyes, you saw yourself. You saw your soul – naked and lost, consumed with arrogance and selfishness. You fear the emptiness, Mr. Tressler, a life without real purpose beyond the pursuit of money. You fear the darkness of loneliness. Who loves you, Mr. Tressler? Whom do you love?"

Tressler stammered, "I have friends, ya know. I do."

The woman looked at him, raised her eyebrows, and said scornfully, "I don't think so, Mr. Tressler, I don't think so. The saddest part is that you expect Benjamin to fix you, to make you feel better, to fill a hole that you refuse to fill yourself."

Tressler had no rejoinder. She was right, of course. It had nothing to do with gratitude or feelings of inferiority. Benjamin, the gentle giant, did scare him; scared the shit out of him. Tressler couldn't get the man out of his mind. The woman hit the nail on the head: his life was empty, devoid of real human contact, or the powerful effect of love. His charm and sociability were a mask, a sham, just a part of a deal, a deal he had made with the devil in order to succeed. Relationships were just levers to open doors. There was no feeling. In fact, he didn't really know what it meant to be happy, or sad for that matter. His life was theater, a series of daily one-act plays, and he played all the parts – hero, victim – it didn't matter. He had played so many that he had forgotten who the real person was. "I still want to see him."

"Yes, Mr. Tressler, I know. Come, it is not too much further."

They walked for another thirty minutes. Neither of them spoke. They turned a corner down a dead-end street lined with tin-roofed shacks. At the very end of the street was the dingy garage-like structure that he remembered when he emerged from Benjamin's house the week prior. At the same time, Mrs. Mashaba stopped and pointed, "There Mr. Tressler, there is Benjamin's home."

Suddenly, Tressler became frightened. He wasn't sure why. Hadn't Benjamin saved his life? Treated his wounds?

Fed him? *What was there to be afraid of,* he thought to himself. But there it was, fear.

The woman knew; she sensed his anxiety. "It's too late to back away, Mr. Tressler. Benjamin knows you are here; he waits for you."

Now, Tressler began sweating profusely; his mouth was so dry, he couldn't swallow. He felt his heart pounding, and he began to shake. Suddenly, all he could see was the garage at the end of the street. Everything else around him disappeared as if he had suddenly acquired tunnel vision. It was more than fear; it was terror. At that moment, he wanted to turn and run, but he seemed frozen in that spot.

He felt Mrs. Mashaba's hand take his. A picture, yellowed and faded, of his mother, appeared, taking his hand so many years ago when he began to cry on his first day in school. "Don't be afraid, my darling Paul. Come on, I will take you to the door."

"Thank you, Mom…er, ma'am, Mrs. Mashaba."

☥

Chapter Twelve

Even before the woman knocked on his door, it opened. Bongani Okonjo, Benjamin, filled the entire doorway. Tressler looked up and, for the first time since his first encounter, appreciated the sheer size of the man. Mrs. Mashaba said something in the Zulu language and bowed her head. She then turned to Tressler, "Mr. Tressler, Benjamin, the Sangoma, has asked me to wait here." With that, she turned and sat on a rickety bench just outside the garage door. She folded her hands on her lap and closed her eyes as if in prayer. Benjamin motioned to Tressler to enter.

Tressler looked around the dark, dismal interior of his surroundings. The first thing that came to mind was the smell. He remembered what felt like endless days lying on the bed, the pain, being fed by Benjamin. Mostly, he remembered the sense of isolation in the darkness. Or was it tranquility? For those lost days, he was truly alone, with only his fears to keep him company. But then, with Benjamin's continuing presence and care, the fear seemed to melt away, replaced with a sense of peace. True, he was alone, but he also felt safe. Benjamin interrupted him.

"Come, Mr. Tressler, sit." Benjamin fell silent, waiting.

Tressler had come this far but couldn't find the words to even start the conversation; some banal comment, perhaps, but nothing. There was only silence. Tressler could feel his heart thumping against his chest.

"Why did you save me, Benjamin?" blurted out. It was the best that Tressler could do as his opening gambit.

"I have already told you: to save your life."

"Yes, but why?"

"Must there be a reason for one man to save another?"

"Yes, Benjamin, there has to be a reason. No one else comes to rescue another at the risk of his own life. You didn't have to come to my assistance in that dark alley, but you did."

Without looking at Tressler and without any sign of emotion, Benjamin said, "We are all connected Mr. Tressler. Every creature that lives and breathes under heaven is connected. It is that irrational connection which compelled me to help you – nothing more than that."

"You're a hero in my book, Benjamin."

"No, Mr. Tressler, I am only Bongani Okonjo, a man who, like you, lives and breathes."

Tressler felt emboldened. The conversation had started, and he wanted desperately to keep it going. Something inside him compelled him to come here and see this through. He wasn't certain why any longer. Maybe, it was the need to equalize his relationship. He was not accustomed to being beholden to anyone. Maybe, in some bizarre way, Benjamin was the channel that would help him find answers. But, to what questions?

"Please call me Paul."

After what seemed an eternity for Tressler, Benjamin spoke. "Paul, you still have not told me why you are here."

"How can I repay you, Benjamin?"

"You cannot. The connection between us is the air that we breathe. It cannot be measured or reduced to a transaction. If that is why you are here, Paul, you have wasted your time."

"I only wish to show you my gratitude for what you did; for the incredible risk, you took for a complete stranger. Isn't that part of the connection you are speaking about?" Benjamin was seated at the opposite end of what served as a table – something that once served as a workbench. It struck Tressler as strange. Although a very large man, Tressler expected this giant to have a booming voice and a commanding and intimidating presence. But, now, as Tressler looked more closely, Benjamin seemed somehow smaller; no, not smaller, but diminished. He noticed that the big man even seated loomed large over the table, but was slumped over. His large head was hanging down, and his eyes were closed. When he spoke, it was above a whisper. There was a long silence. Tressler continued to look at Benjamin, squinting in the dim light, trying to make sense of what he was seeing: a robust man who took on three men now appeared almost frail. Suddenly, Benjamin started to cough; he quickly took a handkerchief from his pocket and covered his mouth. The coughing continued unabated and seemed to be getting worse. It was so fierce that it forced Benjamin to double over.

Tressler walked hesitatingly over to Benjamin, who put the handkerchief in his pocket, but not before Tressler saw a large amount of blood on the soiled cloth. "Are you ill, Benjamin?"

Benjamin picked his head up to look at Tressler, who was now standing in front of him. A thin, wry smile crossed the big man's face. He looked long at Tressler and then uttered matter-of-factly, "I'm dying."

Tressler was stunned. How could this be? This mountain of a man shouldn't be dying. From the moment Benjamin rescued him in the alley to being nursed to recuperation, it was Benjamin's strength that impressed him, not just his obvious physical strength but also his other strength – a deep and silent one. It was like a bottomless pool. It was his strength of principle and conviction, the mix of detachment and generosity, his self-awareness and his selflessness that radiated from Benjamin. But in Tressler's mind, men like Benjamin don't die. They don't become pathetic and weak.

And then it hit him; the real reason he was here, why it was so important to find this man. It really had nothing to do with being beholden to this man who rescued him in that back alley, nor with gratitude, for that matter. It was Benjamin's unyielding, uncompromising and quiet strength that he wished he had. Tressler remembered his own father, a man not unlike Benjamin who possessed the same unbending and tough-mindedness, yet softened with an equal mix of gentleness, which, however, remained hidden from him. And like his father, it seemed to Tressler that Benjamin had closed off a portion of his life, the side that was approachable. It was that side that would have encouraged Tressler to come to his father to share his fear of failure; to help him discover who he was; or maybe, just wipe his nose when he did fall. The tragedy was that his father had died before Tressler was able to penetrate the veil that hid the love he so longed for. And with Benjamin, he had had an encounter with a person who possessed the same attributes. In Benjamin, life was giving Tressler another chance to pierce that veil, and discover the warmth and caring side of his father. But, once again, it seemed to Tressler that fate had conspired to prevent him from taking that journey with Benjamin, and make a discovery that had for so many years eluded him.

"Dying? Why? What's wrong with you?"

"Isandulela gculazi"

"Wha…?"

"It is what you call HIV."

Chapter Thirteen

It took Tressler several moments to absorb what he had heard. He stood dumbstruck, looking at Benjamin, who was having another coughing fit, spitting up blood.

"Isn't there anything that they can do? HIV is treatable. There's no reason for you to die."

"Perhaps, but the Isandulela is too far advanced."

"Why did you wait so long for treatment? It didn't have to come to this?"

"I long to join my wife and my children."

"You had a family? What happened to them, Benjamin?"

Before he could reply, he put a hand over his mouth as he doubled over to cough again. He held his other hand up to signal Tressler to wait for his response. Tressler just stood there shaking his head.

After several minutes, Benjamin caught his breath. He wiped his mouth across his sleeve, took a deep breath and began to speak, but struggled with every word. "They died – 16th June; my beloved wife, Nomusa (Grace), and my daughter, Mbali (Beautiful Flower), were killed during the riots in Soweto in '76. They were among the innocents just crossing the street, so full of life, and the source of my joy. And then, they were gone, like ashes blown in the wind." He fell silent. He looked off into the distance as if remembering those horrible scenes and seeing their faces. For a brief moment, a small smile crossed his face; then his eyes filled with tears. He caught himself, and immediately bolted upright as if some unseen force had struck him.

Given Tressler's ignorance of global affairs, he could not know the enduring pain and personal agonies of those innocent souls caught up in the violence on that dark day in June. What had started as a peaceful student protest became a bloodbath that stained the national conscience for generations, brought global condemnation and implanted a deep-rooted anger that would last generations. Twenty thousand black students protested a government decree that made Afrikaans and English the mandatory languages for all children in South Africa but specifically relegated the indigenous languages – Ndebele, Sotho, Xhosa and Zulu – only for religious instruction, music, and physical culture.

"A waste; my two beautiful flowers wasted, and why?" Benjamin answered his own question, "Because they, the whites, wanted our children to speak only Afrikaans and English. And for that, more than a thousand children, children, Paul, were killed or wounded during this horrifying period." Benjamin looked plaintively at Paul, the pain forever etched in the deep lines around his dark eyes. All the sorrow and agony of 40 years ago was still an open and festering sore that could never be salved.

Tressler couldn't understand it, but he wanted to know more. He could feel that Benjamin had become a shadow, anchored in this penumbra and unable to move without his "flowers." Benjamin turned away from Tressler as tears flowed down his cheeks.

The dam that was Benjamin burst. Between his heaving chest and a flood of tears, he repeated again and again, "And then, they were gone; like ashes blown in the wind, like ashes blown in the wind.

"It was Mbali's sixth birthday. It was going to be a special day. Nomusa needed to shop for dinner. She was going to prepare sweet cakes for our baby. Nomusa asked me to come with her to help her carry the shopping, but I told her that I could not as I had to complete the repair of a car the owner wanted ready on that day. I remember to this day her final words to me, 'My sweet, Bongani, husband of mine, you are always working. Take a few moments away from the grease, and walk with us. The fresh air will be good for you. But, of course, I know my dearest that you cannot. You are always working for the four of us, and for that, you shall always be my hero, my love.'

"I especially remember my beautiful baby on that day. She wanted me to go with them to the market, and when I said I could not, little Mbali, gave my leg a hug, and then ran off with her mother."

"My Nomusa and Mbali were just crossing Mooki Street on their way home from the markets. As they crossed, the police fired into the crowd of students. Nomusa was struck in the head and died instantly; Mbali was trampled to death by the crowd fleeing the police.

"It occurred to me moments after they left that Nomusa had said 'the four of us.' It took me a few moments to realize what she meant. She was pregnant, Paul, she was pregnant. On that day, I lost the three keys to my happiness, to my only fulfillment in life. And then, they were gone, like ashes blown in the wind." His voice trailed off, "…like ashes blown in the wind."

The silence blanketed the dark room. It felt like a tomb; for Tressler, it was almost suffocating. He needed to breathe, or else he thought he would drown. He needed to say something. "Benjamin, I can only imagine your pain, but that was 40 years ago."

"No, Paul, it wasn't 40 years ago. It was only a moment ago; it is happening now. They die in front of my eyes every minute of every day – for 40 years." Benjamin had closed his eyes; he covered his face with both hands; his head was bowed and his shoulders slumped.

Chapter Fourteen

There was not more that Tressler could do or say. Leave the poor man to his thoughts, he thought. "Good-bye, Benjamin." He then turned and opened the door. He saw Mrs. Mashaba sitting on the bench in the same prayerful position as he had left her. Her eyes were closed, and her head was bowed. Her hands were clasped together. It seemed like hours ago. So much had changed. The woman sensed Tressler's presence.

"So, now you know."

"He's dying, Mrs. Mashaba, from HIV."

"No, young man, he died 40 years ago, and he has been dying over and over again, every day since. HIV is merely his escape channel from the real agony. It is his path to them, to his flowers."

Mrs. Mashaba and Tressler walked the entire distance back to Pimville Square, neither speaking a word. They spotted Zukile, who was standing in front of his taxi waiting for them.

As Tressler approached, Zukile glared at him and said stonily, "I will take you back to your hotel."

Tressler turned to Mrs. Mashaba, "Thank you. I do appreciate what you did." Even as he said it, he thought that he really meant it. That was a first for him, and even more surprisingly, it felt good. Then, as if he were watching outside of himself, he gently raised the woman's hand and kissed it. "Thank you."

Zukile didn't say a word on the drive back, and for Tressler, the stony silence was an opportunity to sort through the jumble of feelings after his meeting with Benjamin. Zukile pulled up to the hotel, and without turning around, he said, "Good-bye, Mr. Tressler."

"Look, Zukile, you were right. I have only been thinking about myself. I was a jerk."

Zukile turned to look at Tressler, and it seemed to him that there was something different about the American. Tressler had changed in some way. He could hear it in his voice, or maybe, the expression on his face, but either way, there was a change. Zukile's expression softened, and he said gently, "You have been touched by the Sangoma, Mr. Tressler. Your life will never be the same. I wish you well."

Tressler got out of the car, and Zukile pulled away. Tressler stood in that spot well after the taxi had disappeared from view. He turned to enter the hotel lobby, and as he did so, the ubiquitous doorman reached for the door and saluted him, "Good afternoon, sir."

Tressler stopped as the man held the door open. He could feel the cold air rushing out the door. In the weeks that Tressler had been in and out of the hotel, the same doorman had opened the door for him and greeted him countless times, but he had never noticed anything more than the man's faux-safari outfit. Now, Tressler looked into the man's eyes, and for the first time, saw a person behind those eyes. It seemed to Tressler that the eyes did not convey sadness or anger, joy or sorrow. Here was a man doing a job, a thankless one at that, but doing something that was putting food on a table for himself, and perhaps, a family. His job was to stand in the broiling sun for 8 to 10 hours with a glass door between him and the air-conditioned escape reserved for the wealthy on the other side and offer each person passing through, a cheery greeting. Moreover, he did it without evident complaint or disdain for the guests.

He looked at the doorman and said, rather commanded, "Come inside out of the sun."

"Sir?" came the confused reply. It was the first time that anyone had spoken to him."

Tressler said again, "Come inside."

"Yes, sir."

"What is your name?" Tressler asked.

"The young man jolted in surprise. All he could say was, "Sir?" He had never been asked his name before, and certainly not by any of the hotel's guests.

"Your name," Tressler said. "What is your name?"

"Uh, well sir, my name is Xolani, sir."

"What does your name mean in English?"

By law, everyone in South African schools had to learn English. The doorman hesitated for a few moments. "My name means 'peace,' sir."

"Thank you, Xolani. Hmm." As he entered the cool lobby, he muttered for the first time he could remember. "Wait here, Xolani. I'll be right back."

"Yes, sir."

After a few moments, Tressler re-appeared, holding a plate of fruit and a large glass of lemonade. Tressler motioned Xolani to a chair and offered the man the fruit and lemonade. "This is for you, Xolani. If anyone questions why you're sitting here, just tell them that Paul Tressler invited you to sit here."

"Thank you, sir, thank you."

Tressler smiled, "You're welcome. Enjoy." Tressler turned toward the elevators. Before entering, he took a last look at Xolani, who waved at him. Tressler looked quizzically at himself in the elevator's mirror, "Hmm, what's happening, Tres?"

♀

Chapter Fifteen

Tressler sat motionless on the edge of the bed. He had drawn the drapes; only a bedside lamp lit the room. He felt leaden. At one point, he tried to get up, but found that his legs were too heavy. Thoughts came to him like blinding flashes: a family destroyed; Benjamin's descent into emotional and physical disintegration; Mrs. Mashaba's premonitions; and Zukile's biting criticism. Had his life been nothing more than a shallow puddle that would evaporate without a trace? Was he nothing more than a superficial narcissist whose life was a constant search for self-aggrandizement at any cost? In the end, what was the sum of his contributions? How many people had he used and abused on his path to success? How many lies, half-truths had he employed to gain an advantage, to achieve his goal: wealth, and all that it could buy? Had he really succeeded in life? And, what was success anyway? So long as he was in pursuit of his goal, he didn't have time to define success. Weren't money and success the reverse and obverse of the same coin?

The questions kept coming – faster than he could construct an answer. In fact, that's all he had: questions. He had spent so much of his life living his father's dream that he hadn't taken the time to frame life's basic questions, no less the answers for himself.

He remembered that his father had been born into grinding poverty. His father's father – Tressler's grandfather – was an abusive drunk who died tragically when Tressler was a child. His father's mother was an embittered widow who remained distant and cold until her dying day. Tressler's father struggled, directionless, through adolescence and adult life. There was a flirtation with homosexuality, an inability to form friendships, sexual self-doubt, and fear of failure. Life could be short, harsh, and always, a hair's breadth from homelessness and privation. Tressler, Sr. would find his purpose in life through the unrelenting pursuit of money, status, power and independence. This was the path to success. He passed this formula on to his son, Paul who had been living his life using that roadmap without question or hesitation. Until now, that is.

He couldn't remember how long he had been sitting in that position. His head was throbbing, and his shoulders and back ached when he tried to move. His thoughts were interrupted when the bedside phone range. He felt shooting pains when he finally reached over to answer the persistent ringing.

"Tressler," he squawked.

"Paul? Is that you," said the voice on the other end. Tressler recognized it as Janice Wagner.

"Yes, Janice, it's me. Sorry, I was taking a nap. It's been rather hectic here." Tressler's voice was uncharacteristically soft, and Janice heard the change in tone.

"Are you alright? I've been trying to reach you. It's been days since I heard from you. I've been so worried about you. I've left messages with Reception and the Concierge."

"You did? I never got 'em."

"I miss you. It's been very quiet here without you."

He thought to himself, *worried about me? Miss me? He had never had anyone, certainly not in his office, ever say that to him. How do I respond? Should I?* He took a deep breath, held it for a moment, hesitated, and then uttered just a bit above a whisper, "Well, ….I miss you too."

Janice Wagner had been working with Tressler for the past ten years as his assistant, his chief of staff, and advisor. Although she had a master's degree in finance, she had something else that Tressler valued, and relied on: her visceral understanding of how the market worked; and an uncanny ability to "smell" a good deal. Tressler trusted her above anyone in his business. Janice was more than the 'power behind the throne' as was whispered behind her back in the office. She was also a very good judge of character, especially Tressler's. She heard his reply but for a moment couldn't believe that he had uttered those words.

"Miss you too?" He was such a guarded and buttoned-up personality.

That prompted, "Are you sure you're okay, Paul? Aren't you done with that deal yet? Why don't you come home? I can reschedule your flight."

"Thanks, Janice, I have some things I need to do. I'll be okay, thanks for asking. I'll give you a call shortly." With that, he hung up, leaving Janice perplexed, and in a near panic. She had never heard him speak this way. *He sounded so different, so out of character. Was he on drugs; drunk, perhaps? Or was it something else? What was happening in Johannesburg, she thought? And why was he still there?*

Janice had just turned 35. She was taller than most, nearly six feet, and a former basketball star in college. She was youthful, energetic, and possessed an inquisitive mind. Notwithstanding having graduated top of her master's class, she found that getting a job on Wall Street was more akin to trial by combat. In part, she met the usual sexist resistance to women in the shark-infested waters of high finance, but also to fierce competition from the hordes of new graduates from every country on the planet that saw Wall Street as the quick ticket to wealth. Men were attracted to her, but her intellect frightened all but the most secure; and those with that degree of self-confidence and maturity were few and far between on Wall Street. It was her intellect, wit and fearlessness that came across in her interview with Tressler, who hired her on the spot. After ten years with him, she had achieved her financial target, and was rumored to become president of Tressler's business in a forthcoming reorganization. She had a luxurious penthouse apartment at the foot of Wall Street overlooking the East River. Beyond her all-consuming job and her morning jog with her Jack Russell, "Toodles," her social life was limited to the constant whirl of cocktail receptions, charity events and conferences. She was happy with her life, healthy and well-adjusted. She saw a part of her role was to run interference for Tressler, or when necessary, carry the ball herself. For this reason, her relationship with him was intense. They were together constantly, and were seen more often as business partners rather than as a superior and a subordinate. She had become accustomed to his brashness and hard-charging style. So, it struck her as odd, and even worrying, when the tone of their brief conversation had changed so dramatically. She couldn't put her finger on it, but she sensed that there was some upheaval, something that would turn everything in his life, and hers, upside down. All she could do now was wait.

Chapter Sixteen

Tressler woke up when the chambermaid knocked on the door announcing "Room Service." He found himself lying on the bed, fully clothed.

"No, thank you. Later."

Then, there was silence. The room was dark, shielded from the light by the heavy blackout curtains. He could barely see beyond his extended arm. It suddenly felt more like a tomb than a luxury suite. He felt like he was suffocating. His breathing came in rapid, short bursts. Is this what it's like to drown? Instinctively, his hands went to his throat. He could feel the healing knife wound on his neck. He nearly fell off the bed as he reached for the bedside lamp that then crashed to the floor. He threw off his clothes, clawing at his throat, stumbling, and running to open the curtains. The light exploded into the room, and he jumped back as if struck by lightning rather than sunlight. He ran into the shower, sat down on the floor and let the water play over him.

He didn't remember how long he had been sitting under the shower. He felt like he was floating on his back with his face up to the sun, hands and legs spread eagle, and breathing slowly. It was warm and peaceful as he felt the warm water caress his body. He was a child again. His parents were watching him from the sandy shore at their lakeside cabin. His mother sat under a large umbrella to protect her alabaster white skin. She wore her signature large, blue floppy hat that nearly obscured her small face. She worried about her son. Although he was physically strong, and could play the rough and tumble with the other boys, she knew that he was fragile in so many ways. He was a passionate child, given to bouts of extreme depression contrasted with wild exuberance. Tressler's therapist had suggested Bipolar Disorder that Tressler dismissed as "crap". At a young age, he had sought strong and intense friendships, only to have his overtures repeatedly rebuffed. The truth was that his intensity frightened children of the same age. He found his young friendships disappointing and unfulfilling. He became wary of committing himself for fear of being hurt, and had begun to retreat into himself, spending increasingly more time in his room alone reading, which consisted of everything from Aristotle to Milton Friedman, the economist.

In the silence of his room, and from the corner of his mind's eye, he could see his father, Paul Senior, standing knee-deep in the pool, arms folded, watching over his son doing endless laps under his father's critical review. The young Paul was his first son, and his father's pride and joy. He had great plans for his son, plans that he had had for himself, but were never realized for reasons beyond his control owing to a negligent education system for immigrant children; parents ignorant of their new homeland, and soul-crushing poverty. He had been born into a late nineteenth-century ghetto that was an inhumane holding pen to contain impoverished and ignorant immigrants who would be used to do the work that the established society felt was below their station, and then brutally discarded to wither and die. But it was on the forgotten backs of these immigrants who were relegated to rat-infested slums that the economy grew and prospered.

The young Paul didn't know it yet, but he would learn later in life that he had acquired his father's passion for the success-or-die ethic, an ethic born of his father's suffering in those New York ghettos. There were no half-measures; his father was all in. No one should be content merely to learn to swim, play baseball, shoot, or study. No, you had to be the best at everything – first place. Anything less made you a loser, a failure, and failure wasn't an option for Paul Tressler, Senior. His son, Paul, would succeed where he could not. Failure was a metaphor for another generation confined to a ghetto.

Suddenly, in the distance, he could hear another voice as if it were coming from a cupped hand. It was unfamiliar; harsh, and it sounded urgent. "Mr. Tressler, Mr. Tressler." But it was the knocking on the bathroom door that startled him out of his reverie. The voice behind the door and the banging continued unabated. The door burst open, and two very large hotel security staff rushed in, followed by the chambermaids.

The first person slipped in the pool of water that was now rushing out of the bathroom into the corridor, and cascading to the floor below. Tressler had been lying over the drain. The security man went down hard, and struggled to get to his feet only to slip again, complaining loudly about his back, and shouting to Tressler to get up. The second security man jumped into the shower, and manhandled Tressler to his feet, and in doing so, cleared the drain that Tressler was covering as he lay in the shower.

The security guards mumbled something in the Zulu language about these stupid Americans; and the chambermaids giggled at Tressler's pale nakedness. The women passed towels and a bathrobe to Tressler. The security guards turned and left, and could be heard sloshing through the corridor, cursing.

Tressler stood for a few moments without moving; his arms were at his side and his head hung low. He seemed lost. The chambermaids stood opposite him as if waiting for him to fall over. After long minutes of silence, he began to come around. He lifted his head, and looked at the two, puzzled women.

"I'm so sorry; I just didn't realize…" as his voice trailed off. He wandered into the bedroom, dragging his feet, sloshing through the saturated wet carpet. Just as he sat on the edge of the bed, the bedside phone rang; it was the hotel manager wanting to meet to discuss "…the cost of the damages."

"I'm so sorry, sir. Of course, I'll pay whatever the cost." There was a long silence on the other end as the manager, who was obviously preparing for an argument, was perplexed by the readiness of the American to make reparations.

"Thank you, Mr. Tressler. We will revert to you with an accounting, but in the meanwhile, let us arrange for a new suite." The manager hung up, shaking his head, but grateful that he could go home without acid indigestion. Tressler lay back in his bed, and promptly fell asleep. After clearing up as best they could, the chambermaids sloshed across the room, and left.

Another knock on the door awakened him. This time, it was the hotel porters together with the chambermaids to collect his things to another room. After getting him settled, Tressler, still in his bathrobe, saw that it was already late in the afternoon. This new room faced west; Tressler saw the sky glowing with reds and oranges; long shadows ran the length of the courtyard below. In the distance, he could see the dim outline of downtown Johannesburg. His mind wandered as he thought of the weeks that he had spent in South Africa. How long had he been here? He wondered. He tried to make some sense of it all. So much had happened – profoundly different in a way that he couldn't grasp; frightening, and yet…yet, something that was like a fire was starting to burn in his soul. He looked in the mirror. Yes, things had changed; his face seemed to have aged; his eyes looked tired, and his skin had taken on a sallow hue despite the South African sun and heat. Yet, there was something else, something inside that had been locked away since he was a child, something he couldn't explain, but it was there all the same. He shook his head as if the shaking would fling the thoughts away, but all he succeeded in doing was aggravating his already pounding headache. Before turning away, he said to the face staring back at him in the mirror, "You look like shit."

♀

Chapter Seventeen

He sat on the edge of his bed to watch the last light of the day retreat into darkness. With each passing minute, stars began to glisten in the distance like a handful of diamonds cast on black velvet. The lights of distant Johannesburg came alive, creating a radiance that spread across the horizon. Tressler stared into the distant luminosity, wondering what his staff in New York were doing at this very moment: probably enjoying a steak and a martini to celebrate yet another financial windfall. It occurred to him suddenly that all he was, and would ever become, was nothing more than the sum of a return on an investment.

It had satisfied his colleagues; it gave them the wherewithal to acquire all the trappings of material success. They had the big house, the second trophy wife, and private schools for the kids, and any number of dalliances with young college graduates. Was this his destiny too? Was this what it was all about? Was this the definition of success? Was this happiness? And, would he travel the same path?

Then, it came to him, not in some Buddhist flash of enlightenment, but rather a ball of light that started as a glimmer, then kept growing. It came to him that what was eluding him was something larger than a simplistic, formulaic definition of success, for happiness. It wasn't the big house, the bank account or the number of trophy wives. It wasn't an exalted position in some corporate hierarchy, nor the adulation of peers and subordinates. And yet, the answers still eluded him; but, somehow, he knew that there were answers; they were just beyond his reach. He also concluded that the answers were here in Johannesburg, not in New York.

"Benjamin!" he said aloud. "I need to speak to Benjamin."

With that, he jumped up, and rummaged through his files that had been strewn about by the maids upon his relocation to the new room. Eventually, he found the number he was looking for, and dialed.

"Zukile? This is Paul, Paul Tressler. I need your services for tomorrow. Please, are you available?"

Zukile hesitated for a moment before answering. He recognized the voice, but there was something different. It was the tone, yes, the tone. It wasn't the usual belligerent, arrogant style. The tone was softer, and for the first time, he had used the word, "Please."

"Yes, mnumzane, I am available," Zukile replied without emotion.

"Please, Zukile, call me Paul, and I wish to see the Sangoma. Will you take me there?"

Zukile knew then that something was changing within the young man. He was right. Tressler had been touched by the Sangoma. "Yes, Paul, I will be happy to take you to Mrs. Mashaba. Your visit must begin with her."

"Thank you, Zukile. Will it be convenient for you to pick me up tomorrow morning, say 9:00 AM?"

"I will see you then, Paul. In the meantime, sleep well. I think you are going to have a big day tomorrow. Good night."

"Good night, Zukile, and thank you, again."

♀

Chapter Eighteen

Tressler saw that Zukile was waiting for him when he exited the hotel. He got in the front seat with Zukile. "Thank you for coming on such short notice. I'll pay you the same rate for the day."

"I have already called Mrs. Mashaba. She will take you to the Sangoma."

"Thank you, Zukile, I really appreciate your doing this for me."

They drove in silence through the narrow streets and alleys of Soweto. Tressler looked out the window, seeing, for the first time, the dilapidated, ramshackle houses these people called home. As they slowed to negotiate the street, he could see, and understand their desperation, the anger, and the cynicism at the leadership that had promised reconciliation, reconstruction and renewal, but had only delivered short-term palliatives – a new school here and there, a library, and a medical facility, but there remained the barrier – an institutionalized wall cemented by corruption and racism. However, it was the children that impressed him. He could see them playing soccer, oblivious at this point in their young lives to the hopelessness, anger and frustration that would soon infect them like a disease without a cure.

"Just a few more minutes, Paul," Zukile announced. Tressler's heart began beating faster, his mouth felt dry, and his "thank you" sounded raspy.

They saw Mrs. Mashaba standing on the corner of Modjaji and Modoaba Streets.

Zukile parked the car, and they walked toward her.

"Thank you, Mrs. Mashaba, thank you for arranging the meeting," Tressler croaked. He was now visibly shaking as he extended his hand to the woman.

She looked into his eyes, and smiled warmly. She took his sweaty hand in both of hers. "You have been touched by the Sangoma, Mr. Tressler. Are you ready?"

Tressler hesitated. "Yes, I'm ready. I need to see him."

"Very well, then. Let us go. He is waiting for you." Gesturing to Zukile, she said, "Zukile, you should wait here. I will return him here to you." Zukile nodded, and turned toward his car.

They walked in silence for most of the way. The woman finally spoke. "What is it that you wish from the Sangoma?"

"I don't know, Mrs. Mashaba. I…I just need to see him. I don't know that I want anything. Maybe, just to sit with him for a while, I guess."

When they got to Benjamin's home, the door was already open. Mrs. Mashaba gestured for Tressler to go in. She again took her position on the bench just outside. Tressler hesitated at the entrance. Although it was late morning, beyond the door, it was pitch black. It suddenly seemed like he was stepping into a cave. He could hear his heart beating; he began to sweat; he found it hard to swallow. He was frozen in place.

Then, from within the blackness, he heard a deep voice, "Come in, Mr. Tressler, I've been waiting for you."

He stepped in, but couldn't see anything. "Here, Mr. Tressler, I'm here." He followed the low rumble of the disembodied voice, and when his eyes had adjusted to the darkness, he saw a large hulk directly in front of him.

For a moment, Tressler was speechless. *Why am I here? What am I looking for? And what can this dying man do for me?*

"I…I don't why I'm here, Benjamin. I'm sorry. I should go. I'm sorry to have disturbed you."

"Sit, Mr. Tressler, come sit here with me." Benjamin gestured to the chair that was immediately in front of him. It was a strange tableau: two figures resembling looming shadows facing one another with their knees almost touching.

"What is it that you seek, Paul?"

Tressler could hardly make out any of the man's features; the voice seemed to be coming out of the darkness. Tressler found the disembodied voice at one and the same time menacing and comforting.

"I don't know, Benjamin; I just wanted to be here. Maybe, I'll find answers; I just don't know."

"Answers? But what are the questions? It is the questions that are the beginning of your journey. Find the right questions; and the answers will reveal themselves."

"I am not certain that I even know the questions, Benjamin, but I do know what those questions feel like."

The dark shape that was Benjamin remained silent. Tressler could hear Benjamin's breathing - waiting for him. The air in the darkness was thick and sweltering. Tressler took a deep breath, but it felt like he was under water drowning. His breathing came in short bursts. His head began spinning. He put his head in his hands, and murmured softly, "I don't know, I just don't know anymore. I'm coming apart. Help me, Benjamin, please. I just don't want to feel this way anymore."

He realized that for so many years, he did not own his life. He had traded his soul to the devil of success at all costs. He had put his life in the hands of users, people who consumed his energy – who saw him as a tool. It was really these cunning operators who set the rules that he accepted without a challenge. It was these actors who owned him, controlled him. He had sacrificed his dreams, his freedom for others' dreams, needs and expectations. He had lived outside of himself. He had never taken the time to build an inside self. He was now only a shell: a rich, good-looking, successful businessman, feared by competitors, and supported by obsequious, selfish employees - admired only for his success, but an empty shell. There was no one who would miss him in his absence; no one who would cry if he died. There wasn't anyone who truly needed him. He had become a chameleon – he had changed his colors to suit the needs and desires of others. He had no substance, no immutable and unshakeable truths that defined him.

Tressler felt Benjamin's large hand rest gently on his shoulder.

"Why did I do it, Benjamin? Why did I give away my life? And what have I got in return? I've got everything a man could want, but yet I have nothing. I have no love, no convictions, no sense of belonging? Why?"

Still, Benjamin said nothing.

"Benjamin, help me. Say something!"

The Sangoma broke his silence, "You have found the questions, Paul. Now, only you can come to the answer."

"Is it that simple? Is that what you did when your family died? Did it help to know why they were killed? Did it help you to live in peace? They died, Benjamin. That's it. The "whys" – are they that important?"

Tressler could hear Benjamin take a deep breath. He spoke slowly, painfully. His voice was filled with sadness that colored every word. "Yes, they died; that was an undeniable fact. My mistake – your mistake as well – was not to ask why it happened. Like you, I tried to live with the answer, but instead, it started a path to a slow and lingering death, a death that I live every day. It was the death of my spirit. And, in the course of that spiritual death, it led to what I am now – the living dead. Years later, I did ask myself, 'Why?' Yes, the question was, "Why did the white powers, our slave masters, steal our lives – my family - our land, our future and those of our children?"

"So, you knew the question; what was the answer?" Tressler pressed.

"Fear, Paul, fear of the black man. It was a primal fear that haunted them at night in their dreams. Combine fear with ignorance and power, and the result is death by enslavement, murder, or apartheid. Yes, I now had both the question and the answer, but I was powerless in the face of such forces. So, I raged. I screamed. I wanted to take that anger, and turn it into violence. It consumed me like a fire in the African bush that consumes everything – good and bad – in its path." Then, suddenly Benjamin stopped.

There was a sepulchral silence for what seemed an eternity. Then Benjamin spoke.

"I did commit violence, Paul, but not to others – just to myself. The fire of my anger destroyed my body, my mind and my spirit. So, here I am – dying by inches – and spending those last measures with you, Mr. Tressler. What do you make of that?"

"Are you still angry, Benjamin?"

"Too late I realized that anger is the same poison as the black mamba snake. Once bitten, the death of the soul follows very quickly. No, Paul, my anger is dying with me. What remains now is my sadness from the waste of my life.

But you, Paul, you have found the questions that torment you. Why you have squandered your life for your father, your family and friends, your business, your employees, and your church? That is the real question that angers you, yes?"

"Yes, Benjamin, it is. You're damn right it is! I have had to live my life by everyone else's playbook. And now, when I have the time and money to make my own rules, they call me selfish and narcissistic, untrustworthy and unethical, cynical and a serial sexual abuser.

"I was denied a childhood, Benjamin, unable to do the kinds of things that kids do because they're kids: play football, hang out, go to a movie; you know, just kid stuff. Playing was for other children; I watched them from my window, laughing and enjoying life. But not for me; I was the first child. I had to carry the banner of an entire immigrant family, including aunts and uncles. Other children, my cousins, came along, but it was still my burden to bear. They were absolved of any such obligation. I had to succeed so my father could show the other immigrant families in our all-Italian neighborhood that my family was on the road to success – financial success – in their adopted country. Second place was a failure. Success was all that mattered, Benjamin. My life path was mapped out even before I was born.

"I lived by rules I never understood; rules that were made by institutions that didn't know me; that didn't care about my confusion and pain as a child; that didn't have the time, nor the desire to teach me anything other than blind obedience to rules. Family, church, school, military – all the same: Do your duty, fulfill your obligations in silence, 'be a man and get on with it.' Fun was the path to failure; it was for the 'weak-minded,' my father would say.

"I haven't succeeded, Benjamin, I managed to escape, at least temporarily. The alcohol, drugs, promiscuity have made the escape easier; it helped me live with the anger. People say that I am privileged; that I should be grateful because my family and these institutions gave me purpose and direction. That's bullshit, Benjamin. You know what they gave me? They gave me the gift of guilt, fear of failure and an obsession with success at any price, regardless of whom I hurt along the way. You want to know the truth? Yes, it is a mamba snake's poison, as you say, but I had learned to live with that deadly snake, day after day. It made sense; it helped to shield me from any feelings of pain that love and friendship often bring. I was happy within the hard shell that I had built. I can't be hurt, any longer Benjamin. Yes, the mamba's poison may be flowing through my veins, but it's a helluva lot easier than being disappointed. Maybe, my father was right after all. Love and friendship are for the weak-minded.

"And so, here **I** am, Benjamin, a hollow man, sitting here with you; spilling out my guts to a stranger, but a man who, for no reason whatsoever saved my life, nursed me back to health, and fed me. I don't understand, Benjamin. I still can't understand why, Benjamin. You, Benjamin, you started this…I was fine until you came along. I want to be angry with you, to hate you, for just being you. Why did you do this, Benjamin? Why didn't you just let me die in the back alley?"

Benjamin sat like statue in the darkness. Tressler could hear his labored breathing. Benjamin's words came out slowly: "I know our paths would cross, Tressler, I knew that you were the one."

"The one? The one to do what."

"You will be a Sangoma; one to bear witness to my end, and to your beginning; my people will see me in you."

"Benjamin, are you joking? I'm a New York banker. I'm no healer, a mystic, or a shaman."

"I have waited for a person who has seen, and felt the depths of anger, desperation and spiritual death – like you, Paul. And, it is only such a person who can rise from those depths, who can recognize it in others, and then help to lift them from despair and death. I lifted you, Paul. I took you from your worst moments. I saved you, because I saw you in the mirror of my soul. I could not die without saving you first. You are my redemption for all the sins I have committed. I wasted my life in self-pity, anger, and self-destruction, but you, Paul, you can change all that. You can rewrite the imprints on your soul, and bring hope to the despairing. You must help me through my approaching darkness; and then together we will see the light."

"Benjamin, you don't know what you're asking. I can't do it. I can hardly manage my own affairs. How in the hell am I going to lift others from their despair? And, perhaps, you have forgotten, my friend, but I am white. It's not like people here are going to see me as their great hope."

"You are not white; you are not black. You are a Sangoma. People need Sangomas. There are many in the world – men, women, all different skin colors, and different cultures. Remember Mrs. Mashaba's adage, 'Parsnips and Eggplants.' You will be a good Sangoma; you will be one of the best. I know this."

"Benjamin, I don't know even what a Sangoma is. What does he or she do? I'm not a Jesus, Moses, Buddha or Mohammed. "

For the first time he could remember, Benjamin laughed, "No, Paul, nothing so grand. A Sangoma is none of these. He or she possesses the heart, the wisdom, and the unselfish willingness to take the hand of a person who reaches out to you."

It wasn't one of those startling moments of clarity or a burst of religious enlightenment. It started more like a kernel planted in a large open field, and quickly grew. It wasn't about gratitude really, was it? Neither was it reciprocation, or some sense of obligation on his part. No, neither was it some instant friendship. There was something else. He realized that he and this black man, although complete strangers living in different worlds, were connected; connected in some inexplicable way. He was suddenly certain that this connection was to be a mutual fulfillment of their destinies. This was the person who took Tressler's outstretched arms pleading for help; and it was Benjamin who was waiting for his own salvation from the desolation, from the agony of separation from his beloved flowers. He too had come to realize that he needed to make a human connection to fill the void of contact since the loss of his wife, daughter and his unborn child.

"Wait here."

Tressler heard Benjamin chuckle. "As you can see, Paul, I do not think I will be going anywhere."

Tressler called out to Mrs. Mashaba. "Please, Mrs. Mashaba, will you stay with him for a while? I need to make some arrangements."

He met Mrs. Mashaba at the door. When she looked at him, she smiled broadly, and nodded her head. It struck Tressler as strange. She never looked at him that way before, and certainly, never smiled before. "Of course," she said softly.

Tressler hurried off down the now familiar alleyways. Whereas before, he felt the harsh stares of the residents, this time, strangely enough, they looked at him differently, he thought. Yes, he could feel the difference. Some nodded in his direction; one person even smiled, but most seemed to just accept his presence.

Parsnips and Eggplants – now he understood! Sure, he could explain it with the usual platitudes: equality, diversity, etc. But, this awakening, awareness – whatever – defied logical, moralistic explanation or a definition for that matter. On a level that was just yawning in front of him, he understood. No, it wasn't "understanding." It just was that simple: "Parsnips and Eggplants."

♀

Chapter Nineteen

He found Zukile sitting in his car asleep. The radio was broadcasting a football match between Pretoria and Durban City. Tressler reached in, and gently touched the man's shoulder. "Hey, Zukile, wake up. You're missing the game."

"Bah, they're both rubbish. My taxi driver friends and I could beat them."

"I need to get back to the hotel first. We'll make several other stops, and then back here. It's going to be several hours, at least. Can you do it? I know that you want to get home to your beautiful wife."

Zukile sighed, "Well, if it's that urgent after seeing the Sangoma, then, I will do it, but you will need to explain this to my wife. She thinks you are leading me into a life of sin." He thought about that a bit, and then said, "But she does not complain about the money. Ah, women!"

"Tell you what. When this is over, why don't you and your wife join me for dinner? That should help."

"I will tell her that as soon as I walk in the door tonight. That should help keep the peace for a while. Come, let us go."

Paul Tressler's private phone rang once; Janice Wagner picked up, sounding breathless, as if she had sprinted 100 yards to pick up. "Paul, is that you? My god, where have you been? I was ready to call the South African police. Please tell me you're ok. Everything's going just ok, but we need to have you back here. It's just not the same. I…I'm scared…"

"Janice, Janice, slow down. I'm ok. I'll be back, don't worry. But I need your help."

"Yes, yes, of course, anything. What do you need?

"I need for you to send me a complete kit for in-home patient care for treating someone with HIV."

"What? Do you…"

"No, Janice. It's not for me. Listen, I haven't got much time. Please, call the HIV support group in New York, and ask for a list of all the equipment one would need to care for a patient in the late stages of AIDS. And then buy it, all of it, no matter the price. Ship it by air. Whatever the cost, expedite the delivery to my hotel. Please, Janice. Just do it. Now. I'll explain later. Thank you. I'll see you very soon."

Tressler hung up, grabbed several small bottles of vodka from the room fridge, and hurried through the lobby to Zukile. "Ok, Zukile, next stop is a supermarket in Soweto; one that delivers. Do you have those in Johannesburg?"

Zukile rolled his eyes, and shook his head. "Paul, this is Johannesburg, not some mud hut village in the bush."

"I'm sorry, Zukile, I didn't mean to…"

Zukile interrupted, "It's okay. I understand. You should know that there is a world outside of New York."

"You're right. Sorry."

"There are Shoprite stores in the area," Zukile responded. "My wife shops in those stores. If she goes there, you can rest assured it will be acceptable."

"Okay, let's go."

Zukile looked at Tressler who now sat in the front seat. "I think you're forgetting something."

"What?"

"If this is all for the Sangoma, do you know whether he has a refrigerator?"

"Oh, I forgot about that. No, I'm sure that he doesn't have one. And, I don't think he's connected to his own electricity."

Zukile laughed aloud, "My friend, it is very clear that you are not married."

Tressler screwed up his face in a mock gesture of pique. "Very funny. Okay, change of plan. Let's go buy a fridge… and, I guess, a generator."

Zukile and Tressler spent the day negotiating with appliance and generator dealers. After over paying for an all-in-one deal with same-day delivery, Tressler and Zukile found themselves sitting in a rickety van with a nervous driver who complained of the heat, the drive into Soweto, being over-worked, underpaid, and fearful that he might not make it home that night.

"Mon, why do you want to go there? You are white and rich. You are crazy, mon. They are thieves there. They will steal everything in this truck, and then kill us before we make the delivery."

Tressler looked at Zukile, who just shook his head in resignation.

"I don't think so," Tressler said with a smirk.

"You are a fool, mon; and you, my black brother, you should know better. You are both dead men."

Zukile turned angrily to the driver, "Sekwanele! Le ndoda liye labusiswa yi Sangoma."("Enough! The man has been blessed by the Sangoma.")

The driver's eyes widened like communion wafers. "The Sangoma…?"

Zukile put his hand on the back of the driver's neck, "Wena abesabi kusukela iSangoma ukwedlula amasela uma phi hlungu ehlelwa le ndoda."

Tressler interrupted. "Zukile, whatever did you say to him? He looks terrified."

Zukile had a hard look on his face as he pointed out a street to the driver with his hand still on the driver's neck.

"Zukile, what did you say?"

"I told him that you have been blessed by the Sangoma."

"That's it? And that made him look like he had seen a ghost?"

"Well, not exactly, I also told him that he had more to fear from the Sangoma than the thieves if any harm befell you. It could mean an eternity in the nether world."

Zukile directed the driver to stop in front of the food store. "Paul, let us stop here."

Zukile then turned to the driver. "Linda lapha. Khumbula lokho Nginitshelile. Qapha lo ngempilo yakho." ("Wait here. Remember what I told you. Guard these things with your life.")

Tressler didn't need to ask for a translation. The driver kept violently nodding his head even after they left the van.

As they entered the shop, Tressler said, "Zukile, I have no idea what to buy."

He shook his head, "Yes, Paul, I knew that." He kept turning his head left to right until he saw her walking down one of the aisles, and then broke into a broad smile. "Ah, there she is, my beloved, Thabisa."

The young woman was pushing a food trolley that was piled to overflowing, and pulling another half full behind her. She waved to Zukile who rushed over to her, and took the carts from her.

"Come, Paul, Thabisa has done all the shopping for you, my friend."

Tressler saw the stunning young woman who could easily have passed for a runway model. She was tall, slender as a wraith, and held herself with an air of grace and elegance. Her ebony skin and nearly bald head glistened under the store lights, and showed off her beautiful floor-length dress with green, yellow and black patterns. Her dazzling smile and large round eyes were warm and welcoming. Zukile rushed up to her, and kissed her on the cheek. By contrast, Zukile who also stood about six feet was older, carried a good deal of weight — the result of years driving taxis. The taxi driver could hardly contain his pride. "Look, Paul, is she not the most beautiful woman?"

Tressler smiled, embarrassed. Before he could respond, Zukile gushed, "And, she is as bright – intelligent – as she is beautiful."

Thabisa smiled gently. Her voice was soft and velvety, "Hush, you silly man. My apologies, Mr. Tressler, he is starting to sound like an old goat."

Tressler, normally ready with a quick rejoinder, was at a loss for words when he looked at the shopping trolleys. "I, I don't know what to say, Mrs. Kekana…thank you."

"You are most welcome. I understand that this is for the Sangoma who is quite ill. It is your intention to bring this to him, to care for him, yes?"

It hadn't struck Tressler until the young woman uttered the words, "…care for him." He tumbled the words over and over in his head: "…care for him." What was he doing? He looked away for several moments and then back to her, "Yes, Mrs. Kekana, I guess I am going to care for him."

"I have bought all the food and bottled water I could think of: soaps, house cleaning supplies, books, personal necessities, and of course, sweets. You will need this and more over the course of the next weeks." As if she was seeing the dawning realization in his eyes, she looked intently at him, "This is a great thing you are undertaking for the Sangoma."

Tressler paid for the supplies, which took several members of the shop to load into the waiting van, accompanied by a great show of thanks from the manager who had come rushing out of his office to see the knot of people who surrounded the cash register as the sum for the merchandise grew higher and higher. "Thank you, sir, thank you, for your purchase. We are here at your convenience. Any time. Thank you, thank you," gushed the manager.

The three piled into the van sitting amidst the refrigerator and generator as they made their way to the Sangoma. They drove through the Soweto streets, now crowded with people walking home from work. This mass of people overflowed into the streets where old buses, taxis, and cars were each vying for space, and accompanied by horns blaring, and people shouting curses at near misses. By the time they reached the alley that led to his ramshackle home, it was late afternoon. The sun had now cast long shadows that made the dilapidated homes look bleak and uninviting.

Tressler broke the silence, "Thank you, Mrs. Kakana, for helping. I know you are busy with work and your studies."

She turned to him, "I am happy to help. It is for the Sangoma; it is a worthy thing. And, please, call me Thabisa."

"Well then, Thabisa." Tressler thought for a moment that her name sounded like music. He started again, "Thabisa, I'm grateful for your help."

When they pulled up to the entrance to the alley, they saw a crowd of people standing in silence. The van driver began to shake with terror. Even Tressler became apprehensive. He thought, *what if they are going to steal the food, and kill us?* Zukile felt the man's anxiety. He looked over to Tressler, "Don't worry, Paul, they are here to meet us, and help bring the supplies to the Sangoma's house."

"But how did they know?" Tressler was surprised and confused.

"Everyone knows, Paul. Probably, everyone in the township now knows what you are doing."

Before he could ask how such news had traveled so fast, Tressler's concern evaporated when he saw Mrs. Mashaba open the rear door, and reach in for a bag. Without a word, each person grabbed a carton, a bag or box, and in single file, led by Mrs. Mashaba, walked down the alley to the home of the Sangoma, known as Benjamin. Tressler, Zukele and Thabisa brought up the rear.

♀

Chapter Twenty

As each person reached the door of the Sangoma, they placed the goods down, and softly uttered, "Sala kahle," ("Peace Be With You"), then disappeared into the deepening afternoon shadows.

When the door opened, Zukile and Thabisa, dropped to their knees in reverence to this unique man known all over the Soweto Township as the Sangoma. Benjamin looked at the pile of food, refrigerator and generator, and walked painfully toward the two people who were cowering in his presence. He put a hand on each of their heads, "Thank you, children, may you be blessed with many children." He walked over to Mrs. Mashaba, and gently touched her cheek. She held his hand against her face for a moment as tears welled in her eyes.

Tressler stood, amazed and bewildered at the beautiful tableau. Benjamin then turned to Tressler, and for the longest moment looked deep into Tressler's eyes. A feint smile crossed the Sangoma's lips, followed by a whisper that no one heard. "Yes," Tressler nodded and smiled. Yes, indeed.

For the next several hours, the Soweto residents made several trips carrying the abundance of food, clothes and hardware into the tiny converted garage that Benjamin called home. Zukile wired the generator that finally jumped to life after many curses and bruised knuckles. Tressler tried to make himself useful under the direction of the two women. Benjamin sat watching with quiet amusement as his once Spartan room was now filled with food stacked against the wall. The warm glow from the lamps purchased by Thabisa and powered by the humming generator had transformed the dingy garage into a cozy home. For the first time in anyone's memory, Benjamin's hardened, pained face seemed to reflect the warmth surrounding him.

His face glowed, and his eyes crinkled as he smiled at the constant stream of activity orchestrated by Mrs. Mashaba and Thabisa.

Mrs. Mashaba looked over the now-transformed room with satisfaction. Thabisa walked over to Benjamin, knelt in front of the Sangoma, and with bowed head, offered, "Ahlonishwe Sir, (Honored Sir), May I have the honor of preparing dinner for you?"

In between heaving and coughing, Benjamin rasped a soft, "Yes, thank you, my child."

She jumped to her feet, and rushed to find an empty carton that she used to prop his legs, followed by a blanket to cover them. "Ahlonishwe Sir, this may take a while. You should be comfortable in the meantime."

While Zukile served as a sous chef, and all-around go-for, the young woman began to prepare a feast for the ailing Sangoma. After two hours of non-stop movement, and the clanging of pots and pans, the foul-smelling greasy garage was now filled with the mouth-watering aromas of kota (a white bread stuffed with available ingredients), mogudu (tripe), chicken feet, giblets, dombolo (steamed bread) and chakalala (beans, onions and garlic in red tomato sauce). The aroma wafted into the street, attracting neighbors who began to congregate outside the Sangoma's door.

Tressler could only watch from one side with a mixture of amazement and confusion. Benjamin motioned to him. "Come, Paul, sit beside me."

Tressler remained struck by the overwhelming adoration being shown for this man. As he sat down, he turned to Benjamin, "These people, they revere you so. What is it about you? I know you're a good man; you saved my life for no reason, but this, this is worship. Who are you?"

"I am not a god, Tressler. I am just an old, dying man. I have seen and suffered much in my life, but I am now beyond the hatred, the prejudice and the fear. I can no longer be hurt in this life. My body and soul have now begun to lift into the sky for their final journey. It is there that I shall fulfill my longing for my dust to mingle with that of my beloved wife and children. And then, my journey will be complete. My life, and the travails I have withstood have given these oppressed souls around you the courage, the will, to see beyond their own struggles.

They find a moment's peace in my peace – this is why they are here. Can you not feel their fleeting joy, Paul, a pause from the indignities, and the humiliation they suffer? That is why they are here; why they linger – for a brief 'Ukuphunyuka enokuthula.' How would you say it? Yes, a peaceful escape. This shall be my legacy – a peaceful escape. Until my final moments, it sustains both them and me."

Tressler looked at Benjamin, completely perplexed. How could he possibly understand? This wasn't just foreign to him. He lived in a totally different dimension. His life was a blur of flashes – of blinding energy, like lightening in a stormy sky. One either harnessed that energy or died. His kind were the lightning rods who thrived on the energy; they sucked the energy out of their surroundings, all for one end: self-aggrandizement, wealth, status, and like lightning, absolute power and control. The people in this humble, converted garage were the ashes of those who controlled the lightning bolts. These souls were the ruins strewn about by faceless, soulless, power gods who maintained their grasp on that dominance by herding this mass of black humanity into degradation, exclusion, including physical isolation into concentration camps known as Soweto.

And yet…here they were, happy, singing a Zulu song, "Shosholoza", and then breaking spontaneously into a "Tshwane", a typical Zulu dance.

Benjamin could sense his confusion. "See them, Paul, see their happiness expressed in their song, and the Tshwane. Their bodies are here, but for a brief time as they prepare our dinner, their spirits now mingle with the pure spirit of Africa. They are inhaling the vast African bush, and feeling the primal joy of its inhabitants." Benjamin swept his arm around the room, "This, this house, this broken town, is merely existence, my young friend. It is out there, in the African plain, where our people find their freedom. They may live, work and die in this miserable place; or they may live in other parts of the world, but the spirit of Africa, the dust of the bush, is in their souls. And wherever they fall, wherever their lives end, their dust will mingle with the dust of the African plain."

Tressler said nothing. Benjamin began uncontrolled coughing; blood dripped from his lips, and his face contorted in pain. Thabisa rushed to him with a warm cloth to wipe the sweat and blood from his face. She stood there with a tortured look on her face, waiting for instruction from the old man to ease his pain. "Thank you, child, thank you. It will pass." As if to assure her, he beckoned her to come close, and then whispered in her ear, "How did you know that all these dishes, especially the tripe, are my favorites? May I taste some?"

Thabisa nearly jumped off the ground, such was her hurry to fulfill his wish. She scooped up the tripe, and rushed back to him. His arms were hanging limply at his side, which she took as a signal to feed him a mouthful. He ate the morsel slowly, eyes closed, savoring the taste. Despite his pain, he raised his hand and gestured for her to lend an ear. "It is delicious, child; as good as my wife's."

The young girl stood up, put her hands to her lips, and with tears in her eyes, turned back to the kitchen. For a moment, Zukile looked alarmed, but Mrs. Mashaba put a gentle hand on the taxi driver's arm. "Those are tears of joy."

After the cooking was completed, the table was moved to Benjamin as he found it increasingly difficult to move for more than a few moments at a time. All of the dishes were put in front of the Sangoma, who first tasted each dish, and then passed it to Tressler, who in turn passed it to Mrs. Mashaba. Zukile sat at the opposite end; Thabisa sat next to Benjamin on the other side of the small table. The conversation was warm and familial. It was a gentle time.

Benjamin asked each a question, and then listened intently as his guests responded, only interrupted by the cough that caused Benjamin's face to contort in pain, and occasionally spit up. Thabisa hovered over the Sangoma. With napkins and wet towels, she preserved his dignity at the head of the table, and ensured that his bowl was always full, and wherever necessary, spoon-fed the poor man.

Zukile recounted his days as a taxi driver, citing Tressler as a typical customer – always in a hurry, demanding, and short on tips. Tressler winced, and bowed his head in mock admission of guilt. In between large mouthfuls of kota and tripe, Zukile regaled the table with several stories of the more colorful fares who occupied his taxi: the Indian movie star who insisted that his taxi be fumigated before entering, and then lighting joss sticks; the American business consultant who had Zukile drive to the

McDonald's on Pritchard Street every evening for dinner; and the Russian tourist who hailed him at the Johannesburg Park Train Station, and asked him to drive to the City of Durban in order to go shark diving. A few moments into the journey, the Russian asked how much further; Zukile informed him that they were only 27 minutes into a five-and-a-half hour journey of 338 miles. Without a word, the Russian jumped from the taxi at the next stop light, leaving his suitcase and diving equipment in the taxi.

Waving his fork and knife in a moment of excitement, the taxi man said between mouthfuls, "These are nothing, sir, as I come home to the real prize in my life, my beloved Thabisa."

Despite the deep lines in Benjamin's pained face, he scowled, "She is not a prize, my son, that you have won in the bazaar. She is your future. She is the foundation upon which you can build a life. Without her, you have nothing. She is not a prize, but a treasure like no other."

Zukile bowed his head. "Yes, sir, I understand. Thank you."

Mrs. Mashaba spoke in a low, almost prayerful voice, in the presence of this special man, the Sangoma. She spoke of a husband who also died of the Isandulela (HIV) when he worked the mines in Zimbabwe. It was ten years ago, ten years of constant struggle to raise three children. With little help from equally impoverished neighbors, she worked menial jobs – cleaning toilets, washing floors in the abattoir, and taking in the laundry that she washed by hand. Even as she related this lifetime of hardship, there was a peaceful radiance about her. Her children were grown. Now, she was a grandmother of four. "I sometimes wonder," she said, shaking her head, "which was the more difficult. Were my children slower on their feet than I, or are these little ones who are faster?" The Sangoma replied, "I fear, woman, that it is we who are growing older faster. Our feet serve only to keep us upright; our grandchildren are for outrunning their grandparents. You have lived a life of service not only to your children and grandchildren but also to all of us, Mrs. Mashaba. In many ways, you have been a mother to us all."

Then, Benjamin turned slowly to the young woman, Thabisa. He raised his arm, fighting the pain, to reach for her. Ever so gently, he put his enormous hand on top of her head. For a long moment, he looked into her eyes, and as he did so, tears began to well up in his. She was startled and reached over to him, "Sir, is it the pain? What can I do for you?" She wiped his face with a wet cloth. The tears streamed down, filling the creases in his face. He continued to look at her with a combination of pain and joy. No one spoke a word. A profound silence filled the room.

Only Tressler and Mrs. Mashaba understood... ashes blown in the wind.

Benjamin closed his eyes; he drifted back all those years. He could see her face, Mbali, the little flower, his beautiful daughter. She was smiling and calling to him, "Ubaba, poppa, here I am; I see you."

As Benjamin opened his eyes, now overcome with joy, he looked directly at Thabisa, and said softly, "Ngiyabona kakhulu" ("I see you too"). The young girl smiled. She looked at Mrs. Mashaba and Tressler, and in that briefest exchange of glances, she also understood. She spoke one word, "Yebo." (Yes) Tressler had no idea of what

Benjamin had just uttered, but he knew that the young woman seated alongside Benjamin, the Sangoma, and Thabisa, would be forever connected.

Benjamin looked at Tressler, and then back to Thabisa, "Child, Mr. Tressler, will help make your dream come true. You will be a great physician."

Tressler smiled, and nodded his head.

Benjamin looked over to Zukile, "My son, there is more food here than we can eat. Please take it and distribute it to those who have been sitting outside. Mrs. Mashaba, would you please help him?" Benjamin then took the hands of both Thabisa and Tressler, and drifted off to sleep.

φ

Chapter Twenty-One

Tressler sat motionless, holding Benjamin's hand until he felt the buzzer from his mobile phone. He whispered, "Tressler here."

"Mr. Tressler, this is the concierge at the hotel. We have a rather large delivery for you. The driver will only unload upon receiving your signature."

"Okay, wait a moment, I need to get directions…"

"Excuse me sir, there is also a person, a woman, here who arrived this morning, and is here with me and the driver. She too is looking for you."

"A woman with the driver. I don't understand. What is her name?"

The concierge held the phone out to the woman, "Paul, it's Janice."

Tressler was annoyed. Her place was in the office, keeping the business on track. He felt that someone from his other life, from the dismal grey world, had intruded on this other life. His voice was harsh as he admonished her, "Janice, what are you doing here? You should have just had the equipment delivered. There was no need for you to come all this way. Who's minding the business?"

"I'm sorry, Paul. I have been…we all have been…worried about you. I won't interfere. Just let me see that you're okay, and that you'll be back home before too long."

Tressler's raised voice awakened Benjamin, who had overheard Tressler, and the anger in his remarks to the woman on the phone. He turned to look at him. "Paul, she is here because she cares for you. Why are you so angry? I sense that she traveled all this distance not just to deliver some equipment; that could have been easily done. She came here to see you. I sense more than just a professional responsibility."

Tressler angrily shot back, "That's nonsense. She's an employee, and she had no permission to come here."

"Is it nonsense, Paul Tressler? I believe that you are lost not because you don't know the way ahead; you are lost because you cannot see, or worse, because you are afraid to see what lies in front of you."

"I see just fine. My world is filled with narcissistic, self-centered, shallow people. They care for me only because I'm their meal ticket to satisfy their venality. There's no room in that space for love and friendship."

Benjamin raised himself and swept his arm across the room. "Then tell me, why have you done all this? Am I then nothing more than a channel, a vain attempt at proving that you are not one of those self-absorbed souls? Are you trying to make peace with the world through me?"

"You saved my life; I owe you."

"You owe me nothing. I saved you in that alley because I believe that no one should exert power over another to satisfy one's own selfish needs. I saved you because you are like me, like Zukile, Thabisa, and Mrs. Mashaba. You are part of my family. I owe them nothing, but only to return their selfless love with my own."

Tressler abruptly called out to Zukile, then turned to Benjamin. "I have to go." Benjamin nodded, and started another fit of coughing.

☥

Chapter Twenty-Two

Zukile and Tressler drove back to the hotel where they saw a rather large delivery truck, and a driver sitting in the cab smoking. Zukile went over to the driver as Tressler went into the hotel.

Zukile approached the driver, "Is that a delivery for Paul Tressler?" The driver looked puzzled, and then replied in English. Zukile shook his head. He took that to be a bad sign.

"I've been waiting here for an hour, mon. I have other jobs."

Zukile replied in English, "We need to go to the Soweto district to deliver."

"No, mon, I'm not going there. Too dangerous."

"This delivery is for a Sangoma. There's nothing to fear."

"I don't care if it's for the archbishop; no way, mon."

Tressler was angry; angry with Janice, angry with Benjamin, at the whole damned thing. His mind was a jumble: was it really about selfless friendship and selfless love? Before he could think about it any further, he saw Janice who rushed over to him and threw her arms around his neck.

"Paul, thank God. I was worried to death. I didn't know what to think, especially when you asked for the HIV equipment. I'm so sorry, Paul. I couldn't help it."

Tressler gently pushed her back, and looked into her eyes. She was crying, but smiling at the same time. Was she happy to see me? He knew Janice as a rock-solid deputy who could be as hard-hitting as he was in negotiating deals; and a tough second in command. But here she was, crying what seemed to be tears of happiness. Then, the unexpected happened.

"I'm not sorry, Paul, that I came. I knew in my heart that there was something going on, something that you didn't want to share with anyone in New York. I was afraid that I wouldn't see you again – see you, Paul, you. Some of the staff saw your absence as a signal that our business was going under. I tried to assure them, but I had to come not just for assurances, but to see for myself that you're alive and well."

"I'm ok, Janice," was all that he could muster.

"Well, I know that you're alive, but you look terrible. You've lost weight; and the bags under your eyes are larger than my suitcase. What's been happening to you? Please tell me."

Tressler looked at her for the longest moment. Her eyes were red from lack of sleep and crying. She looked into his eyes. For the first time, he allowed himself to truly feel for another human being. He realized that she had traveled all this way to see him, just him. And for the first time, he was touched. He then put his arms around her, and kissed her gently on her forehead. She put her arms around him again, and for several minutes, nothing was said. He could feel her trembling as he held her close. He was lost in a sudden jumble of thoughts and feelings he hadn't experienced before. He hadn't intended it to happen, but then he lifted her chin, and gently kissed her on the lips. Before he could utter a word, he felt a tap on his shoulder.

"I'm sorry, Paul and lady, but we need to get the van driver to deliver the equipment. He's afraid to go to the Sangoma's home. I think that we are going to need your special power of persuasion."

"You mean money, right?" Tressler.

"I'm afraid so. My personal threats about a curse from the Sangoma didn't work."

"Okay, let's go. Oh, Zukile, I would like you to meet Janice Wagner. She works with me in New York, she's my right hand. Without her, nothing works. Janice, meet Zukile Kekana, formerly my driver, now my friend."

Zukile smiled broadly at Tressler at the change in his status. He turned to the young woman and addressed her first in Zulu, "Sawubona, kuyajabulisa," and then in

English, "Hello, it is a pleasure." He turned to Tressler, "Again, I'm sorry to interrupt, but we must go now. The driver may leave."

"Janice, I can't ask you to do this. It would be more comfortable in the hotel, but…"

Before Tressler could finish, she said, "I'm going wherever you're going."

Tressler looked at her in a way he never had. He smiled, leaned over and gave her a hug. "Okay, then. Let's go."

The driver followed Zukile's taxi to the same street, where they were met again by the group of people who had unloaded the van with food supplies. Again, at the head of the crowd stood Mrs. Mashaba. The terrified driver refused to leave his van while each member of the group carried the medical equipment up the street to Benjamin's house. After completing the unloading, Tressler signed the delivery receipt notice, and passed it to the driver through the narrow crack the driver allowed in his window. As the driver roared off, Zukile muttered loud enough for some to hear, "Moegoe." ("stupid, cowardly – a weakling").

Once again, as each person reached the door of the Sangoma, they placed the goods down, and softly uttered, "Sala kahle," ("Peace Be With You"). Mrs. Mashaba directed operations while the two men grunted and groaned as they brought the new bed, portable oxygen, a respirator, and monitoring equipment into the now crowded garage, which quickly took on the image of a hospital room. Janice had been watching the proceedings with open-mouthed amazement.

When all had been organized and the hospital bed prepared, Mrs. Mashaba turned to Thabisa, who had not left the Sangoma's side. "I think we can help bring the Sangoma to his new bed." Janice rushed over to the young woman. "Let me help you."

"My name is Thabisa," and throwing a nod over toward Zukile, she said, "And that man with the large waste is my husband. Are you Paul's wife?"

Janice smiled at the reference to Zukile, who shook his head in mock indignation and patted his growing waistline. "No, Thabisa, Paul is my boss."

Benjamin slowly opened his eyes when he heard the strange voice. "And, you are Janice, yes? Ngiyabonga ngokwenza kwenu uzothatha uhambo olude kangako."

Janice turned to Thabisa with a quizzical look, "He says, 'Thank you for making such a long journey.'"

Janice noticed that there was something about this large man that was unique. It was an aura that seemed to surround him – not the kind that resembled a gold dinner plate that one sees in a religious painting. Despite his illness, he radiated tranquility and calm. With Thabisa on one side, and Janice on the other, they struggled with Benjamin's size and weight but managed to help Benjamin over to the bed. He held his shoulders back and his head high. Again, with the aid of the two young women, he gently laid back on the hospital bed. It took both women to lift his legs into the bed.

He looked at both women, and with a hoarse voice, he quipped, "Am I not fortunate indeed to be surrounded by two beautiful women?"

Feigning disapproval, Mrs. Mashaba shook her head, "Men."

Tressler turned to Mrs. Mashaba. "We need a doctor, Mrs. Mashaba. We have all the right equipment, but we need a doctor to help us at this point. Do you know of any?"

"Yes, Mr. Tressler, but at this late hour, the nearest clinic is closed, and no doctor will venture into this area, but I am certain that we could find a doctor at the Chris Hani Baragwanath Hospital."

The woman hesitated for a moment as if she were trying to remember a bad dream. "It is one of the largest in the world. It was where my husband died."

"I'm sorry, Mrs. Mashaba, I didn't mean to upset you."

"Thank you. It is a pain that will never heal."

"Will you take me there? I would like to speak to any doctor on call."

"Of course, if you think it will help," she replied.

Tressler turned to Zukile, "Shall we, my friend, go find a doctor?"

Zukile took in a long breath, and exhaled whilst shaking his head in a mocking gesture, "If it were anyone else, Paul, I would say, 'No, it is impossible, but with you, I have no doubt that we will return with the entire hospital!'"

Chapter Twenty-Three

The threesome set off, and with Zukile driving like a man possessed, they reached the hospital in less than 15 minutes – a ride which would have taken double that if Zukile had adhered to traffic signals, and lane markers. Tressler directed Zukile to the Emergency Entrance, and jumped out almost before the car had come to a halt, and set off running, "Wait here. I'll be right back!"

With a sweep of his arm, Zukile shook his head, "He is crazy – all of them are crazy," referring to no one in particular. Mrs. Mashaba got out of the car, and followed Tressler, who had already disappeared into the hospital.

As it was late in the evening, and a weekend, there were only a few patients waiting in various states of distress. Tressler skidded to a halt in front of the duty nurse's desk. Although slight with closely cropped greying hair, her penetrating eyes told Tressler that this was not a woman to be trifled with. He blurted out, "I need a doctor immediately, please."

"What is your condition?" she replied, looking at him skeptically.

"You don't understand," Tressler replied. "I need a doctor to come with me to administer to my friend."

"I'm sorry, sir. We don't make house calls. This is an emergency room for emergencies," the nurse replied sarcastically.

"How about money then, I'll pay double whatever price to a doctor who will come with me. I have a car. My friend is dying. Please, you need to find a doctor – a good doctor."

"Sir," she replied with great emphasis on the word, "**sir**." "Why don't you call a good doctor in the morning," again with emphasis on the word, "**good**." "There are many of them in Johannesburg."

Tressler thought he would try a different tack, "Look, you seem to be an understanding person. My friend has HIV, and is dying by inches as we speak. Isn't there anyone who could come out to check that we have all the right equipment and administer the medications? He's in a great deal of pain, and is bleeding with every cough. It will take only a few minutes, I promise. He needs something for the pain. He is in agony."

The duty nurse rose from her chair – she was taller than Tressler had imagined – came around to face him, bristling. "Sir, do you see those people over there? They have been waiting, some for hours for relief from their pain. Why is your friend different from them? What makes him or her more worthy of medical attention than those poor souls?"

Tressler was about to launch into a scathing attack that may have worked on Wall Street, but would only cause more resistance here.

Just then, Mrs. Mashaba came rushing through the door. It was clear that Tressler, for all his good intentions, was not about to get anywhere with his bullyboy tactics.

The duty nurse turned, expecting to see another patient being ushered in. Her hard face softened when she saw Mrs. Mashaba, whom she remembered when she was a young ward nurse tending to her dying husband. "Mrs. Mashaba, it's so good to see you after so long. Are you in need of care?"

Mrs. Mashaba replied in Zulu in order not to offend Tressler with his good but misguided intentions, "I am fine, thank you, Mrs. Ndosi. Thank you for remembering. It was so long ago."

Linda Nsele had been a nurse for 30 years in Chris Hani Baragwanath Hospital, and had risen from a ward nurse to the Chief of Nursing. As was her custom, despite being the most senior nurse on the hospital staff, she took a turn on night duty to give the other exhausted nurses an opportunity to get away from all the chaos and horror of the emergency room.

Continuing in Zulu, Mrs. Mashaba whispered to the head nurse, "I'm sorry about this man's behavior. He means well. He is, however, here on a mission of mercy." She continued to speak to Mrs. Ndosi in Zulu, recounting the events of the past several days, and the involvement of this unusual man.

For his part, Tressler just stood there with a confused look on his face, and his hands at his side. Why don't they just speak English? He did manage to catch one word: "Sangoma," at the same time, he saw the nurse's face soften. Tressler was about to enter the conversation when Mrs. Mashaba put a gentle finger on her lips – a signal he understood.

Mrs. Ndosi looked at Tressler, then to Mrs. Mashaba, and then back to Tressler. She just shook her head, and shrugged her shoulders as she turned and disappeared through doors marked **"Ngokuqinile kungekho"** **("Strictly No Entry.")** Several moments later, the chief nurse emerged from the emergency treatment unit with a large bag in hand.

"Come, let us go. If the Sangoma is at this advanced stage, I can administer the necessary palliative treatment myself."

Once again, Tressler tried to speak, but was gently silenced by Mrs. Mashaba with a quick headshake and a finger to her lips, re-enforced by Mrs. Ndosi's hard stare.

They found Zukile waiting with an engine running directly opposite the emergency entrance. The ride back to Benjamin's home was equally terrifying for Tressler, whereas the two women seemed unfazed by Zukile's kamikaze-style driving.

***

When the four arrived, they were struck by a serene tableau. The warm glow of the table lamp filled the room, and seemed to surround Janice and Thabisa, who were sitting on either side of the bed, each holding one of Benjamin's hands in their two hands. Benjamin was peacefully asleep. The two young women seemed to be in silent prayer at the same time, counting the big man's slow and even breaths.

Thabisi was the first to speak in a whisper addressing the foursome led by Mrs. Mashaba.

"He is asleep now, but only in between the coughing which I fear is getting worse."

Mrs. Ndosi approached the bed, and looked around at all the monitors and equipment surrounding the bed. "Mr. Tressler, I understand your agitation now. You have been generous in providing all the right equipment, but it is of no use without professional assistance. I am sorry I was so harsh."

"That's ok, Mrs. Ndosi, I guess I came on rather strong. I'm sorry too."

With a sweep of her hand, the nurse said, "Well, then, let us put this equipment to use. Leave it with me for a few minutes." With practiced efficiency, she quickly hooked up drips and monitors; and inserted needles into Benjamin's veins to carry the needed fluids and medication. The others could only stand by and watch. Within a few minutes, she was satisfied that everything was in order. Monitors were humming and whirring and recording vital signs that she noted on a pad. She then took a wet cloth, and gently washed his face. Taking another fresh moist cloth, she wrung the water onto his lips and into his mouth. She then turned to the others, "Make certain that you are clean before touching him. Any infection would be catastrophic for him."

She showed Janice and Thabisa how to wash the rest of his body at the same time preserving his dignity. As the two young women were gingerly washing a respective leg, the fluid drip had its desired effect – Benjamin's eyes slowly opened only to see a group of people with solemn looks, speaking in hushed tones. The two women instantly stopped and backed away. Mrs. Ndosi layed a gentle hand on his enormous head, leaned close to his ear, and said softly, "I am Nurse Linda Nsele from the Chris Hani Baragwanath Hospital, and I have the privilege to treat you, honored Sangoma. I have administered several medications to make you comfortable."

"Thank you, Mrs. Ndosi," came the hoarse whisper, "But you should return to the hospital. There are others who are in more need than I."

"I will ensure that you have a continuous supply of medications during this trying time, honored Sangoma."

With what seemed great effort, Benjamin reached out, and touched the nurse's cheek. "Peace be with you." She took his giant hand and kissed it. She turned, and despite years of experience in a trauma care hospital, then left with tears in her eyes.

♀

Chapter Twenty-Four

With the aid of Mrs. Ndosi, a rota had been prepared to ensure that someone was with Benjamin day and night to monitor his condition, record the readouts, and ensure that the medications were administered continuously. There were so many residents of Soweto who had heard of Benjamin's dire condition that the list of volunteers had to be limited. Paul and Janice, Zukile and Thabisa had taken up residence in Benjamin's garage, sleeping either on the floor or on two donated cots while Mrs. Mashaba divided her time between looking after her grandchildren and taking a turn looking after Benjamin.

One morning, Mrs. Mashaba came with her youngest granddaughter. Dumisani immediately recognized Tressler, and ran over to him, and climbed on his lap to stroke his pale face. He was embarrassed at first, especially when Janice observed wryly, "Oh, Paul, how sweet! She likes you. I didn't know that children were attracted to you."

But she was shocked when Tressler wrapped his arms around the little girl and replied, "Well, Dumisani and I are friends, aren't we, Dumisani?" The girl climbed up and threw her arms around Tressler.

Mrs. Mashaba reached out to take hold of the child, but Tressler shook his head, "That's all right, Mrs. Mashaba. She's no trouble." The infant made incomprehensible cooing and burbling sounds. Tressler laughed and said, "You're absolutely right, Dumisani. It will be our little secret."

Janice could not believe her eyes. "Paul, you understand what she's saying?"

"Of course, I do, Janice. Don't you?"

They were interrupted when they heard Benjamin stir, and call for Paul. Carrying little Dumisani with him, Tressler walked over to his bedside. With one look at Benjamin, the little girl had found another source of amusement. She promptly wriggled out of Paul's arms and onto the bed, where she climbed up and sat on Benjamin's chest, evidently intrigued by all the monitors, and began the same incomprehensible burbling. A mortified Mrs. Mashaba rushed over to the bed, but was stopped by a wave of Benjamin's hand.

"She is no weight, Mrs. Mashaba. She is so beautiful." The words came out slowly and painfully. Nevertheless, she gently lifted the child from Benjamin, and took her outside. Benjamin turned to Paul, "You have done all this for me. I am in your debt."

"I seem to recall, my friend, that when I said the same thing, you replied, 'you owe me nothing.'"

Benjamin's face went soft with a gentle smile, he said, "Ah, and now the student becomes the master."

"I remember, Benjamin, you said to me that we are all connected. Something to the effect that everything under heaven that breathes is connected. You said it was an irrational connection, and nothing more. Well, I think you're only half right. I have come to realize in these few hours and days that you and I are indeed connected. At first, I thought it was nothing other than an accidental encounter in a back alley, but now the connection is no longer irrational. In fact, it's no longer a connection; it's a bond, Benjamin, a bond. You mean something to me, Benjamin. You're important to me. That's why I'm here; and why I'm going to see this through to the end – wherever and whenever that is."

Benjamin reached up, and his massive hand gently touched Tressler's face that now had streaks of tears. Tressler held Benjamin's hand to his face. Benjamin looked into Tressler's eye for several long moments. Tressler sensed that Benjamin was searching his soul, searching for the truth, perhaps. Their eyes were locked onto each other. Neither spoke. The others in the room could feel something extraordinary happening. No one dared move. And then, the big man slowly lowered his arm, closed his eyes, and whispered, "Yes, a bond." With that, Benjamin entered a deep sleep from which he would not awake, but there was a trace of a smile on his face.

Tressler turned to face the others, who seemed frozen in place. He first went over to Mrs. Mashaba and took her hand between his. He gently kissed her hand, and in a soft voice, said, "Parsnips and eggplants. I understand. Thank you." She nodded and smiled. He then went over to Zukile and Thabisa and embraced both of them. "Thank you. You have been loyal and devoted friends to me even though I was a stranger to you." When he turned to Janice, Tressler hesitated a moment – to gather his thoughts. He put his arms around her, and held her close for a very long time without saying a word. He felt her warmth as she drew herself closer to him. He kissed her on both cheeks, and ever so gently on her lips. He looked into her eyes, "Janice, you are important to me in so many ways. I can see that now. I want you in my life. Let's begin here." She simply nodded as her eyes filled with tears, "Yes, Paul, I love you too."

☥

Chapter Twenty-Five

Each morning, Mrs. Ndosi ensured that there was a delivery of medication and saline drips for Benjamin. And each day, there was a continuous stream of people who came to the house to pay a final homage to the Sangoma, Bongani Okonjo – Benjamin - this gentle giant of a man who brought serenity and peace to whomever he encountered. Although seldom seen in public, the community knew he was a presence in their lives, in their homes, and in the mean streets of Soweto. And, every day, they saw the strange white man sitting alongside Benjamin's bed, keeping a vigil. Rumors spread that this "umlungu" – white person – had received the gift of sangoma from Bongani Okonjo, and would be his successor. Impossible! They thought. How could such a thing happen? But yet, there was something about this white man that defied their preconceived notions. He sat alongside the bed motionless, head bowed, eyes closed as if in prayer. Could it be?

Janice did the daily run back to the hotel to ensure that the Tressler business was operating smoothly. Zukile acted as the courier for the medications, and Thabisa was busy with her application to university for medical studies. Her grades in undergraduate classes were excellent, and a prepaid check for tuition and books all but guaranteed her admission. She knew of Tressler's promise to Benjamin, and tried to thank him, but Tressler only smiled and nodded his acknowledgment. After all, he had given his word, but more importantly, Tressler could see in this young woman the future of her country, the future of Africa. What better reason could there be?

Occasionally, Benjamin's eyes would flutter when Tressler spoke to him to give him the news of the daily visitors: Thabisa's university application, Zukile's new business venture delivering food and merchandise into Soweto, and Janice's management of his business – now their business.

As Benjamin fell deeper and deeper into his coma, the expression on his face changed from one of pain to serenity. As Tressler wiped Benjamin's brow, he whispered, "You know, my friend, we could become rich men if we charged admission. I never appreciated how much you are loved; you, the Sangoma. There is now a well-worn path to your bed. All is well here. Rest easy, my dear friend, you have earned it."

One evening, as Tressler, Janice, Thabisa and Zukile were finishing a delicious stew prepared by Mrs. Mashabe, Thabisa noticed Benjamin's hand moving, as if beckoning someone to his bedside. Tressler knew the time had come. He jumped up, and went over and took Benjamin's hand.

"What is it, my dear friend? Are you in pain?"

There was no response, only a final grasp of his hand around Tressler's. The grasp became tighter and tighter. Benjamin's breaths came slower and more labored. At that moment, it felt like a surge of electricity went through him.

Tressler felt the grip become tighter still. His hand nearly disappeared into the big man's grip.

Tressler beckoned for the others to come to the bed. "We are all here, my friend. Mrs. Mashaba, Zukile, Thabisa, Janice and me. We are with you."

Tressler took Benjamin's enormous hand and pressed it against his chest. "It's ok, my friend. Go, go ahead and be with them, your angels. They have been waiting for you. Go with our love."

Benjamin took a deep breath and exhaled slowly, and then nothing. The monitors suddenly screamed out with numbers and lights flashing, signaling the finality. Tressler nodded to Thabisa, who turned the monitors off. There was a deadly silence.

"Goodbye, my dear friend, my Benjamin, Sangoma."

With tears in her eyes, Mrs. Mashaba went to the door to announce to those gathered outside that the Sangoma had passed into the other world to be with his beloved angels. There were sobs and tears for the great man who had provided comfort, wisdom and compassion to everyone who sought him out. Although late in the evening, the knot of people broke out into various Zulu melodies – in their unmistakable harmony – to honor the Sangoma. He was now among the "Amadlozi" – the ancestors.

The singing came to an abrupt end when Tressler appeared in the doorway. Somehow, in these last few moments, he, too, had become larger than life. The crowd turned to Tressler, who spread his arms and began, "My dear friends, our beloved Sangoma has joined his angels, but believe me when I say that his spirit lives on. It lives on in me and in every one of us, in all the living creatures to whom we are joined. His spirit lives on in the African plain, in the cities, and here in Soweto. Do not be sad; be joyful that he shared his love and compassion with all of us." With that, Tressler turned to rejoin the others, leaving the crowd speechless.

Janice sat quietly next to Tressler, holding his hand. He had hardly spoken a word in the hours since his friend had departed. She sensed that there was a raging conflict being resolved. He could feel his life-changing within him by the moment. It felt like a volcanic eruption. The desolation of his present life, and the disappointments and regrets of his youth seem to be exploding, and then like lava, it poured into the sea, cooling and then disappearing into the morning tide. He felt unburdened but still knew that, like the tide, the sea of his doubts and sorrow could return to overcome him. But now he had a starting point: Benjamin, the Sangoma. He would carry the man in his heart like flowers around a trellis. This place had become his safe place, his retreat and the place to rebuild his life.

♀

Chapter Twenty-Six

The funeral ceremony for Bongani Okonjo – Benjamin – the Sangoma was held on a beautiful Spring morning with air redolent of the African plain in the distance. It was a simple affair, reflective of his life, but attended by hundreds of people who had been touched by this giant of a man. The mourners said that death had not rendered him a shadow – an "isithunzi" – in the Zulu tradition to wander aimlessly until brought home to his ancestors – to his "buyusa" – because he was already home with his angels: his wife Nomusa, daughter, Mbali, and his unborn child whom Benjamin had named, "Jabulani."

✳✳✳

As the sweet fragrance of incense curled in the morning air, Benjamin was buried alongside the graves of his family in the Avalon Cemetery in Soweto, surrounded by throngs of people singing a Zulu song of joy, "Injabulo enhliziyweni yami" – "Joy, Joy, Joy, with Joy my heart is ringing."

Zulu tradition requires that only patrilineal descendants of the deceased perform any rituals, thereby excluding non-kin. But it did not come as a surprise to the attendees that Tressler, who stood at the head of the grave together with Janice, Zukile, Thabisa and Mrs. Mashaba, officiated the ceremony when he recited "The Lord's Prayer" which the mourners repeated in Zulu. There were rumors and suspicions that they were in the presence of someone special, Paul Tressler, a reincarnated Sangoma perhaps. Those suspicions were confirmed: the spirit of their beloved Bongani Okonjo had indeed passed on to Tressler, when he finished the English rendition of the prayer with a near-perfect farewell in Zulu: "Okuhle, umngane wami, umfowethu (Goodbye my friend, my brother)."

Tressler then turned to the throng, and spread his arms as if to envelop them, and then said simply, "Benjamin will always be with us in our hearts. His spirit lives on. 'Ngiyabonga.'" (Thank you)

The ceremony was concluded. As each mourner passed Benjamin's ornate casket that was nearly covered with a mountain of African flowers of every hue, some bowed their heads; some said, "Hamba kahle" (Goodbye). Tressler waited for every mourner to pass. Some acknowledged him with a nod; others offered a soft "Ngiyabonga." After nearly an hour, only Tressler, Janice, Thabisa, Zukile, and Mrs. Mashaba were the ones who remained, each momentarily lost in thought. It then began to dawn on them how much time they had spent together over the last weeks. Each had been strangers to the other with never a prospect of the meeting had it not been for an unintended encounter with Benjamin. Now that the focus, Benjamin was gone, suddenly they stood together, almost embarrassed. What did they really know about one another? Why did their paths cross? Was it fate or just an accident? Would a rich white man have done all this for one poor, sick black man had it not been for the confrontation in a dark alley? Would Zukile venture into Soweto if he had not been paid a princely sum to do so? Certainly, Thabisa and Janice would have been cosseted in their ivory towers, oblivious of Benjamin's plight. Tressler sensed the discomfit.

"Come on, let's go back to Benjamin's place, and have a meal. We need to talk, don't we? Thabisa, although I would love for you to cook one of your spectacular dinners, why don't we find a takeaway? Let's just be together for a while – alone together."

Thabisa and Zukile went off to fetch dinner. Mrs. Mashaba, Janice and Tressler made their way back to Benjamin's. When they entered, it had all the appearances of a hospital room vacant after a death. The monitors stood silent; the drips were half used, and the bed sheets still bore the wrinkles from Benjamin's body. It was more a vacated tomb than a home. When Thabisa and Zukile returned with the food, the mood brightened a bit.

Tressler took the lead. "Thabisa, would you do a favor for me, please? Would you contact Mrs. Ndosi, and arrange to have all this hospital equipment donated to the hospital in the name of Bongani Okonjo? Zukile can you organize the transport?"

Thabisa spoke for both of them, "Of course, Paul. I'm certain that the hospital would be pleased by this...And so, would Benjamin."

Tressler turned to Mrs. Mashaba. "Would you accompany Janice and me, Mrs. Mashaba? I would like to purchase some additional furniture." With a sweep of his hand, Tressler said, "I would like to make this place more of home, a home that Benjamin would have liked."

"Yes, I would be pleased to accompany you, but for whom are we buying this furniture?"

"For me, of course," said Tressler matter of factly. "I intend to buy this place."

Mrs. Mashaba's brow furrowed, "But, Paul, your life and future are thousands of miles away. Soweto is not your home. It certainly should not be your second home. I understand your desire to preserve Benjamin's memory, but I don't think this is a good idea."

For several long moments, there was a tense silence. Tressler felt wounded. So much of his life had changed in this room. Indeed, what he had become was in this garage cum house. Why not preserve it, treasure it? Keep it alive, fresh in his memory. Tressler looked around the room, and the faces stared at him, waiting for his reply. The silence was overwhelming for Zukile.

"Paul? My friend, you cannot capture Benjamin's spirit like a child captures a butterfly in a jar. Benjamin's spirit is like the butterfly that now lives in you. You have been touched by the spirit of our ancestors, and they live everywhere: in the bush, in the city, in all of us, and now in you wherever you are.

If you wish to purchase this house, that's fine, but you cannot live here, but because of Benjamin, this is now your spiritual home."

The expression on Thabisa's face said it all to Tressler. He could see the admiration for him, her youthful exuberance – the future of Africa, and her intensity – all written on her face. Janice took his hand, and said gently, "You have a big heart, Paul, and a part of your heart will always be here, but your life is elsewhere – maybe not New York, but it cannot be here."

Tressler was lost in so many thoughts. He closed his eyes, and slowly nodded his head. What would Benjamin do? How would he resolve this quandary as a Sangoma? After all, had he, Tressler, not become a Sangoma as well - just as Benjamin had predicted? Then, it came to him.

"You're all right, of course," he said softly. "I cannot live here. My life **is** elsewhere, but Janice is correct, a part of my heart will always be here with you, and this house." He stopped, but the others sensed that there was more to be said.

"Mrs. Mashaba, would you do me the honor of living here? I'm certain that Benjamin would have liked that his home be fruitful with the sweet music of your grandchildren. It is a perfect place for Dumisami to grow up."

"Mrs. Mashaba smiled. "Thank you, Paul. I would be honored. I could certainly do with more space for my grandchildren. You would always be welcome, of course. It is your home too."

"Well, then, that settles it. Shall we go shopping? On second thought, may I suggest that Thabisa and Janice accompany you? I think it would make it easier for you to shop without the little ones. Zukile and I will look after them while you are shopping." Zukile closed his eyes and shook his head at the prospect. Thabisa chuckled at the thought of her overweight husband chasing after four little children.

Mrs. Mashaba rarely laughed, but this time she did. "Mr. Tressler, do you know what you are asking? Three women shopping for furniture? It could be devastating."

Thabisa and Janice joined in. Thabisa said only half seriously, "Can you afford such an extravagance, Mr. Tressler?"

"After we're through, Thabisa, he will need a second job," Janice joined in.

Zukile could only shake his head, thinking of the work of carrying all that furniture.

☥

Chapter Twenty-Seven

Several days had passed since their last meeting in Benjamin's home. Tressler was back in the hotel suite on a conference call with his staff, getting updates, and much to everyone's shock, asking questions, and giving praise for jobs well done. He promised that he would return shortly, and explain the reason for his extended absence. He thanked everyone for their loyalty to him and the firm, and promised that things would be better for everyone upon his return.

"Hi." Janice bounded into the room. "Let's see: we have completed the furniture shopping; the hospital equipment has been donated per your instruction; and poor Zukile is managing to get the companies to deliver all the stuff we bought. I think I've learned a few Zulu curse words from Zukile. He idolizes Thabisa. Poor man, he will need to shed a few pounds to keep up with her. And, she loves him to death. I guess there's no explaining love. Oh, and by the way, I made reservations for our flights back to New York, the day after tomorrow."

Tressler closed the conference call, and turned to smile at her. "What would I do without you?"

She came over to him, and kissed him square on the mouth, and then said excitedly, "We're having a housewarming party tomorrow night at Mrs. Mashaba's new home, and we're invited! Paul, you will love it. The furniture is beautiful. Mrs. Mashaba has great taste. Thabisa and I were just there to confirm her choices.

I'm starved. Do you think that we can just have a quiet night here this evening? My legs are aching from following Mrs. Mashaba all day."

"Sure, Janice, order whatever you like for both of us," Tressler responded absent-mindedly.

"Are you okay, Paul? Is something the matter?"

"I'm just thinking about going home, that's all. So much has happened, and so quickly. I'm having a hard time processing it." Janice took his hand and gently kissed him. "I think I understand. You've been through a lot; and a lot is changing in your life. Just let it sink in. Take your time."

♀

Chapter Twenty-Eight

It was late in the afternoon as Paul Tressler and Janice Wagner walked down the street to Benjamin's house for the housewarming. The shadows of the small shacks turned the streets prematurely dark. It was by now a familiar walk down the street and alleys of Soweto, and also familiar for many of the residents of the neighborhood to see these two. They were greeted warmly by most, but mixed with a few unpleasant stares. Everyone knew of the transformation of Benjamin's house. For most, it was an act of both generosity and testament to Benjamin by this unusual man; to some, it was a painful, but ever-present reminder of the inequality between white and black South Africans, despite all the talk of reconciliation and promises of new opportunities for all.

When they reached Benjamin's house, they were warmly greeted by Mrs. Mashaba, "Siyakwamukela ekhaya lethu," and then in English, "Welcome to our home."

For a moment, Tressler was at a loss for words. The furniture and decorations were typical of the Zulu culture – with splashes of every color under the sky. The lighting – a change from the light bulb that he remembered on those first few fateful days – cast a warm glow emphasizing the multi-colored armchairs, woven kambas of dazzling hues, beaded wall hangings, and kilima bologan mud cloth and kuba pillows strewn about. In silent tribute to Benjamin, his bed had been converted to a sofa with a soft hand-woven mud cloth throw offset with another stunning array of colorful hand-crafted pillows.

Tressler was stunned. He kept shaking his head as if to reconcile what he remembered to what he was seeing now.

"Do you like it, Mr. Tressler?" Mrs. Mashaba asked.

"Like it? I love it, Mrs. Mashaba! It's fantastic!" He then hesitated for a moment, and said softly, "Benjamin would be proud. You have truly honored his memory." At that moment, Thabisa rushed over to Tressler, and handed him a huge plate of phutu (crumbly maize porridge) and amasi (curdled milk which tastes like cottage cheese). On a side table, he saw sugar beans, stew, and cabbage, sweet pumpkin and boiled madumbes (similar to yams). It was truly a feast.

They ate and drank into the early morning hours filled with both tears and laughter. It was truly a fitting tribute to their friend, mentor and Sangoma, Benjamin. After numerous hugs, handshakes and kisses, Zukile and Thabisa drove Tressler and Janice back to the hotel.

"Thank you, Zukile, Thabisa. Thank you, again for all you've done for Benjamin, and especially for me and Janice. I will never forget." With no further ceremony, Janice and Tressler exited the car, and disappeared into the hotel to begin packing for their journey home.

The next morning, after paying an enormous bill for the room, the damages, the meals and the numerous bottles of vodka, Tressler took his leave. On the way out, he stopped at the porter who was at his dutifully at his post dressed in his oversized faux safari outfit.

"Good morning, sir. Have a good day," the young man said, trying to sound earnest.

"Good morning. Xolani, isn't that right?" Tressler replied.

"Yes, sir. You remembered." The young porter had an astonished look on his face.

Tressler reached in his pocket, and pulled out a wad of South African Rand notes, enough to feed a family for a month, and handed them without fanfare when he shook Xolani's hand. The boy looked down in his hand, but could not find the words in time to thank this white man who had become the talk of the hotel. Tressler had already jumped into the waiting taxi with Janice.

"Paul, where is your luggage?

"I gave it all away to the chambermaids and the security guys. It's the least I could do for giving them so much grief during my stay."

Janice was waiting for an explanation, but given the smile on Tressler's face, none was really necessary.

After a short ride to the airport, and a quick check-in at the first-class lounge, they were about to enter the security gate when they saw Mrs. Mashaba, Zukile and Thabisa off in a corner. They looked forlorn and lost in the frenetic atmosphere of the airport. They walked to the trio, where they were greeted by Mrs. Mashaba, and Dumasami, who had been hiding behind her grandmother. With tears in her eyes, she said, "We have come to wish you a safe journey, haven't we, Dumasami." The little girl came from behind her grandmother, and grabbed a hold of Tressler's leg. Tressler lifted the child and held her close. He whispered in her ear, "I will see you again, Dumasami, very soon, and I will bring you a very special toy." The little girl threw her arms around Tressler's neck and gave him a wet kiss on the cheek. Tressler laughed, and said, "Ah, yes, it works every time." Janice frowned. She could only surmise why Tressler reacted the way he did. The little girl disappeared again behind Mrs. Mashaba. Thabisa put her arms around Tressler. "I can't thank you enough, Mr. Tressler. You've done so much for me."

"I've done nothing more than what you deserve – a chance. Take it. I know that you will make Benjamin, me and all of us proud. One condition, however."

"Anything," she responded.

"Look after him, Thabisa," Tressler said, pointing to Zukile's growing girth. He needs you. Put him on a diet, make him exercise, and stop him from getting so upset with his soccer teams."

Thabisa laughed. "I promise, but it will be difficult on all counts."

Tressler took Zukile's hand. "I could never thank you enough for being there for me; for putting up with me; and for helping me cross a bridge from the darkness. I shall never forget you. You were my first friend. I will always be there for you."

Zukile spoke, "And I will always be here for you. Promise me – us – that you will return someday soon."

"I will be back, Zukile. Count on it. You, all of you, are my family. We are bound together by the spirit of Benjamin. Yes, I will be back. This is not goodbye."

Tressler went over to Mrs. Mashaba. "You have been more than a friend; you have been a mother to me, indeed, to all of us. Without you, all of this would never have happened."

Mrs. Mashaba smiled and kissed him on the cheek. She whispered in his ear, "You possess the spirit of the Sangoma, Paul. It is a priceless gift. Use it for the good of all who come to you."

"I will," was all he could say as he looked into her deep and loving eyes.

Janice and Tressler turned; waved a final goodbye; walked through security; and went on to their flight home.

♀

Chapter Twenty-Nine

They were seated together in a nearly empty first-class cabin. Tressler had hardly spoken a word – only the required "Yes," "No," "Please," and "Thank you." He seemed distant to Janice – somewhere else in his own world.

As the plane lifted off, he turned to Janice, "I feel him inside me. It's a presence. He's here, Janice. Benjamin. He's here sitting with us."

Janice watched Tressler with some alarm. Initially worried, she quickly realized that he was having some kind of internal conversation with the Sangoma.

After several long minutes with his eyes closed, Tressler finally said, "Yes."

He turned to Janice, "Marry me, please."

Janice was momentarily stunned. *Was this typical Paul Tressler: a lack of impulse control?* And yet, it seemed to Janice that this was not so much a momentary and fleeting burst of emotion, but an epiphany, an opening into his world that was morphing before her eyes. The request was urgent, intense, and to Janice, real.

"Yes, Paul," was her simple response.

"Thank you. I'm not sure how to love, or where to start, but I am absolutely certain that I need you in my life, every day for the rest of my life. I didn't realize that until now. I guess that's a start, right?"

"Yes, it is."

Tressler kissed her and felt the warmth of her lips. He lingered as he felt her warm hand on his cheek.

"Great! Let's get married here. I promise I'll be the best husband you ever had." His boyish enthusiasm had returned.

"I've never had a husband before, Paul."

He looked over to a surprised flight attendant. "Captains of ships can marry, right?"

The flight attendant looked at Tressler, not knowing whether to call the on-board security or call the captain. "Well, yes, I suppose, but…"

"And please, give a glass of champagne to everyone on board this aircraft. We're going to have a celebration."

The flight attendant dialed the captain, "Captain, I think you might want to come to the first-class lounge. You won't believe this

About The Author

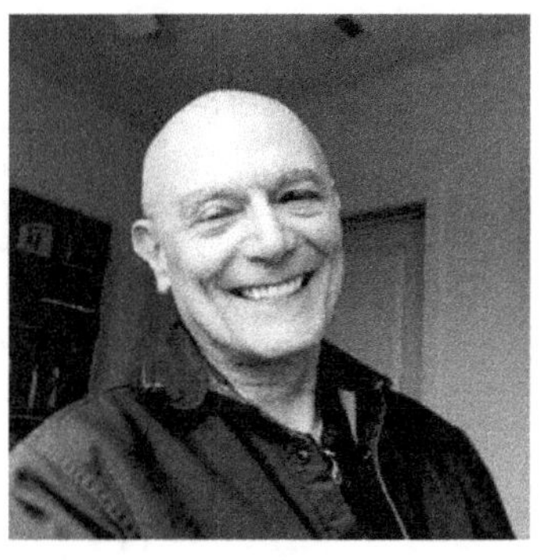 **Philip Antony** has drawn on his experiences from his multi-faceted career as a lawyer, business consultant and university professor. He has travelled the world where he was privileged to meet and interact with people of many cultures, which he has woven into all of his stories. He has produced a long line of young adult stories and adult novels in which his rich imagination and international experiences have created a cast of colourful, relatable characters and exciting adventures.

The underlying theme of his stories is the power of love, friendship and compassion that overcome the forces of hatred and division. Although his stories are works of fiction, his novels convey that contemporary message with excitement interspersed with warmth and humour. His work stands in stark contrast to the enmity and divisiveness we read about in our world today.

www.ingramcontent.com/pod-product-compliance
Lightning Source LLC
Chambersburg PA
CBHW070946180726
48291CB00004B/1156